BEYOND SOLSTICE GATES

Ahelia Publishing

Helena, Montana

War Of the Firmament

By Kimm Reid

BEYOND SOLSTICE GATES

Where
what lies above
and what lies beneath
is nothing
compared to what
lies within

AHELIA
PUBLISHING

Table of Contents

Race Against Time

1

THWACK.

"OUCH!" someone shrieked.

The Travelers had fallen asleep, but they were definitely awake now! How they fell asleep, none could even imagine, for in the deepest dark of the moonless night, everything that could be shaken was being shaken—ferociously.

CLUNK.

"OUCH!" someone else hollered.

Jennifer jumped to her bootless feet.

"WHAT'S HAPPENING?" she wailed. "WHAT'S GOING ON?" Panic set in as Jennifer noticed a good amount of blood on the cave floor and also that the cave itself was beginning to give way. Rocks were falling from above, the ground was shaking from below, and it was making dangerous-sized cracks in itself.

"WHAT'S GOING ON?" Jennifer screamed louder in an effort to wake the others. It worked. Everyone was up now, although Pierce was wobbly and confused. He grabbed his head and whimpered as Bella looked at him and shrieked. When she did, the cave made a *CRAAAAACK* noise and let loose a large portion of one side. The Travelers rushed to the other side to avoid being crushed.

"We've gotta get out of here … NOW," Matt shouted. "IT'S CAVING IN!"

Judah and Matt helped Pierce; he had a gash on the side of his head from the falling rocks. One must have walloped him as he slept.

"I don't remember anything hitting me," Pierce anguished. But then again, if he was asleep, why would he?

"Maybe," Kaija Mae suggested, "the rock hit you so hard it knocked you out, but because you were asleep, you didn't notice." It made no difference if they could come up with a reason or not. It was evident something had hit Pierce on the head; he had a gash, and the blood was around where he'd been laying. They decided it made no difference and let it drop. Besides, there was too much else to worry about and focus on and think of and figure out. Pierce would be fine; the wound wasn't terribly serious, even though his head throbbed.

There was nowhere to go where debris wasn't flying through the air or fires were not sporadically igniting. The king had obviously decided to destroy the land, and that's exactly what was happening. From what the Travelers could tell, it didn't seem like such a destruction would take long to complete, and panic threatened to strike them down if the cave didn't do it first.

Last night, when Miriam had thrown the first of the clay tablets into the sea, the king had been watching from afar and became hopeful that this girl he'd made a blood-pact with was going to save his land. He'd sent word on the wings of the air and put out an immediate decree to halt the destruction. The land had stilled itself—but not for long.

As King Shrailzhar continued to keep an eye on the situation, he became outraged as Leviathan destroyed Miriam. If he was angry about that, it was nothing compared to what he was about to feel. The king's blood boiled within his evil veins as he had watched—and saw the sea spit out the tablet.

When that dreadful sea offered the Travelers one more tablet as a token for handing over Miriam, the king knew there was nothing left for him to do. The only option was to destroy his land, take the stolen souls of the Waiting Ones with him, and flee Trilleah—for good.

In his fierce anger, Shrailzhar had set into motion the land to be destroyed, once and for all—that much was obvious to the Travelers. They were constantly having to duck and dart pieces of debris that were being torn from Trilleah and hurled through the air. It was as though the biggest tornado ever to spin itself into being had come to the Dark Land and was ripping it apart piece by piece. It was not going to slow down its twisting until every stone, every twig, every bush, and every blade of dead grass was ripped apart and hurled into the great abyss.

Neither Pierce nor Jennifer had cloaks, so when pieces of rock or branches or other objects would be thrown into them, they felt it.

"Here," Judah shouted to his sister. "Try squeezing in here with me." He opened one side of his cloak to let her squish under his arm. She moved into the opening immediately.

"Thank you," she wheezed, out of breath.

Bella did the same for Pierce, and so everyone was a bit more sheltered from all that was being hurled through the air. It didn't seem as though the objects were sent intentionally at the Travelers and indeed, this was the truth. The land had no care whatsoever of the Travelers. It was instructed to destroy itself, not specifically those in it. Nevertheless, the Travelers had to work hard to avoid being struck by any of the hurled chunks of Trilleah being tossed to and fro.

"HOW ARE WE GOING TO FIND THE HOLLOW?" Sam bellowed. The winds were howling so loudly now that it was almost impossible to hear any of their shoutings. They had to screech and holler and hold on to one another just to keep from being blown over. If they tried to walk to the left, the winds would rise against them. If they tried to walk to the right, the winds would change direction and become a wall, unable to be broken through. No matter which way they went, that way became the impassible one. They were getting nowhere fast, and trepidation continued to thrash at them from the inside.

The Travelers didn't realize yet—they would soon—that a great battle had risen between themselves and Trilleah. If they were able to find the last tablet and break the curse before the land could destroy itself and own the souls of the Waiting Ones, the king would have nothing left … not his land, nor his kingdom, nor the cursed souls. The king would be finished.

Yes, the battle had begun and it raged hard.

If the Dark Land were to win out, however, and destroy itself before that last tablet could be found, it would be the Travelers who would be without the cursed souls. Their mammas and sisters and fathers and brothers would remain with the king forever.

"OVER THERE," Sam shouted. He was pointing a few steps to the side, where there looked to be a small space notched out of the trees. It would be slightly quieter, and maybe they could come up with a plan to get back to Asphelia's Hollow.

Together, the group of worn and weary Travelers weaved and stumbled over to the spot. They ducked—fell, really—inside and scooted as far back in this tree covered den as they could go. It still rumbled and shook, but at least it was slightly quieter in the den so they could hear one another without screaming.

"How's your head, Pierce?" Bella asked.

"I don't know. It's throbbing, and I'm dizzy," he murmured.

Bella stretched up as high as she could to try and get a look at his head; since the trees were hanging quite low, they had to be hunched over in the den.

"Oh dear," she muttered as she separated his hair to reveal a gash much larger than she'd seen earlier. It was bleeding heavily. Bella looked around to find something to press against it to slow it down, but there was nothing except swirling dirt and leaves. "It looks awful," she whispered to Kaija Mae.

Kaija Mae stood up and moved to where Bella was. The girls began whispering and Kaija Mae began singing her songs. Oh, how blissful they were. She laid her hand over the split in Pierce's head and kept right on singing while Bella continued searching for something—anything—to press over the gash. The color had gone right out of Bella, leaving her horribly pale.

"Are you okay, Auntie?" Jennifer asked. The ones who were watching Bella look at Pierce's bleeding head thought it must be a terrible wound for her to suddenly look so ill. It turned out that Pierce's head was not at all what had made Bella's color slip from her face.

"I just realized something dreadful," she whispered. Nobody wanted to ask what that something dreadful was; nobody had to. Bella kept right on talking, sharing with the others what nobody wanted to know. She went on to explain that she'd realized just now that they were in a race; a race against Trilleah.

"Trilleah wants to destroy itself before we can find the last tablet," she cried. The truth was that it was the king who'd commanded the land to be destroyed and he'd called for all the mighty powers of the air—both seen and unseen—to come and wreak havoc.

Regardless, the Travelers knew the race for the end had begun. They also knew that if the Trows' curse was going to be broken, and if the souls of the Waiting Ones were to be set free, they would have to move fast. They would have to find that last clay tablet before Trilleah could destroy itself … and the tablet … and the Travelers.

"What are we going to do about Pierce's head?" Jennifer asked. "He can't keep going unless the bleeding stops." She snickered because just yesterday she'd have suggested leaving him behind or feeding him to Leviathan. But after the two of them sat weeping together last night on the side of the shore, she saw Pierce differently. She saw him with compassion, as one who *did* have a heart after all—perhaps one of the biggest hearts she'd ever known—but it had been buried under the heaviness of guilt and regret and secrecy. She'd felt him shake and had heard him weep as his heart broke.

"It will be all right," Kaija Mae replied with a wink.

"How?" Bella asked. She was again looking at Pierce's gash, which had nearly stopped bleeding. "What did you do?" she asked. It wasn't conceivable that the bleeding had stopped on its own. She knew Kaija Mae had something to do with it.

"I sang to it," she said.

It seemed ridiculous, but the Travelers were reminded of the time Kaija Mae had sung over Jennifer when she'd smashed her head in the hollow and knew there was undoubtedly something healing in her songs. Besides, everyone knew there was no time to debate how the bleeding had stopped, they were just glad that it had.

"Okay," Matt said. "Now, how do we find our way back to Asphelia's Hollow? Do we even need to go back? Maybe we don't need to waste the time it will take to get there," he suggested.

"Of course, we need to get to Asphelia's Hollow," Bella snapped. She didn't mean to be so abrupt, especially toward the handsome young man whom she admired so deeply, but she was far too upset and downright scared to think of what might happen if they couldn't find their way back to the hollow.

Matt didn't want to argue with Bella, so he remained quiet. He was thinking that the Travelers didn't have enough time to return to the hollow before trying to track down the last tablet, but he wasn't about to say that to Bella, not right now.

First, they didn't know which way the hollow was. Trilleah had become so turned around and upside down and inside out that they didn't even know which way they were going. Second, if they did somehow manage to find their way back to the hollow, the chances it would still be safe were low. None of the Travelers knew much about King Shrailzhar or his land, but it seemed obvious that the first place he would destroy would be Asphelia's Hollow.

Bella had always seemed to know the right thing to do, so Matt decided to trust her to know the right thing to do now, even if he disagreed; and he did disagree. He should not have followed Bella after all, for she was about to lead them into a pit of their own destruction.

"We've GOT to get moving," Pierce said. He was less dizzy now and decided he was okay to step out of this little windless inlet in the trees; back into the demolition of Trilleah.

"There's no more time to waste," Sam shouted as he pulled his cloak tighter around him and yanked the hood over of his wild hair. Bits and pieces poked outside the hood still, and while he looked amusing, none was amused.

"Let's go," Matt added, as he followed Pierce into the chaos.

Judah pulled Jennifer closer and tucked her under his arm. He pulled the cloak as snug as it would go and followed the others out of their shelter. As they stepped out together, the wind caught them, pushing them sharply to the side. Jennifer swung around and her body slammed hard against a boulder.

"Oaf," she grunted as her breath was knocked out of her.

"Oh no," Bella screamed. She was right behind them and saw Jennifer's body slump to the ground as it hit the boulder.

"I'm okay," Jennifer grunted as she tried to catch her breath and get back on her feet. The wind knocked her down again and instead of trying to get back up, she crawled on her belly straight back into the shelter tucked in the overhanging trees.

"Where are you going?" Pierce shouted, but of course, no one could hear him. He turned to head back to the shelter as well. As he did, his head began to throb, and he felt overwhelmed … and responsible … and out of time.

We are never going to make it, he cried in his mind.

You will make it, he heard come right back to him.

Not a Who

2

Now, there was a time not so long ago, when Pierce paid no attention whatsoever to his Shailma, but that was not going to be today. When he was dozing in and out of sleep throughout the night, he was sure he'd heard his Shailma whispering to him—a soothing kind of whisper—not one filled with direction or rebukes or wisdom, but a whisper that provided the boy with a gentle spirit and an untroubled heart.

He remembered thinking as they laid on the cold, hard ground listening to Leviathan screaming as every lightning strike hit him,

"There's no way any of us is going to sleep tonight," but they did. All of them slept soundly … except one.

Maybe it was because Miriam would no longer be cursing their tongues or causing their flesh to burn and swell, or maybe because having one remaining tablet to track down seemed like a doable task. Most likely, however, the Travelers' sleep had more to do with the fact that something was in the cave with them.

Even though handfuls of dust and pebbles and stones were falling here and there, and the floor was rumbling, foretelling of what was to come, they felt a deep comfort. Each one felt the same thing— although there was certainly no time to discuss what that thing was— every worn and weary Traveler felt it just the same.

Whatever it was that lulled them to sleep could not be put into words anyway. It felt as if a big, cozy blanket had been pulled over the top of them; like someone unseen had come and tucked them in.

"Safe as a bug in a rug," Pierce remembered his mother saying when she'd tucked him in so many years ago. Well, she used to say it, before Peter was hit by the car; before Miriam had told the most unforgivable of lies and said he'd pushed his brother. Oh, that dreadful lying girl. For a moment, Pierce was glad she was gone.

Memories of his mother kneeling beside Peter's broken body flashed in Pierce's mind along with the feelings he'd felt that very day as he watched her sob. Wails came over him now, and he worked hard to stifle them, lest the others heard the brokenness trying to sneak from his heart. He shook his head, desperate to get the thoughts, memories, and sounds out of his mind.

Pierce managed to chase all those memories back to the dusty corners where they belonged, for now, but he knew they'd pop up again soon; they always did. For now, he brought himself straight back to the moment, hiding in the small crevice beneath a few swaying trees, and forced himself to stay in it.

"Jenny," he said. "Are you okay?"

"I … I think so," she muttered. "I can't stand against the wind, though," she whined. "I don't think I can go back to the hollow with you. You'll have to go without me …"

There was no way any of the Travelers were about to let Jennifer stay here alone. The chance that they'd have to come back this way to find the last of the tablets was highly unlikely, and they probably couldn't find their way here again if they tried.

It made no sense for Jennifer to remain behind, but she was quite right in thinking she couldn't stand against the winds. With her tiny frame and sock feet and cloak-less body, there was no way she'd be able to stand up against everything the land was throwing at her.

"We need a plan," Matt said.

"A much better plan than we have now," Sam added.

"And we need it fast," Kaija Mae murmured.

There was quiet among them for a moment while everyone thought. The truth, of course, was that nobody was thinking at all. Every one of the Travelers who was hunched and cramped tightly inside the tiny thicket of broken bushes and overhanging branches was listening; listening for any wisdom or direction or thought or comfort the Shailmas may offer for such a time as this.

"Anyone?" Kaija Mae asked. Jennifer shrugged her shoulders. Bella shook her head.

The time is short, Jennifer finally heard. *You cannot stay here, Little One. You won't last.*

What am I to do then? Jennifer asked her Shailma for finally, he had come and whispered to her mind.

Ask another for their cloak, she heard. Surely that couldn't be right. A cloak would only make her more easy to blow around, would it not? Jennifer must have heard Simeon wrong. Then she heard it again.

Ask another for their cloak.

There was no use arguing; Simeon always knew things she did not know, and he never gave her wrong information. Even when she thought he did, in the end, she could look back and see that Simeon was right, and she should have listened. She'd listen this time. Quietly, because she was afraid of the reaction from the others, she spoke up.

"Would anyone be willing to lend me their cloak?" She winced a little inside because she was sure nobody would be willing to give up their cloak, and waited for a tongue-lashing about how selfish she must be to ask such a thing.

No tongue-lashing came. Instead, to Jennifer's surprise, everyone spoke at once, offering her their cloaks.

"Of course," said one.

"I will," offered another.

"Take mine," one more suggested.

She was grateful and took the one closest to her.

"Matt," she said, her voice shaky. Jennifer's memory flashed back to one other time when Matt had removed his cloak. She'd seen him become a vapor and get sucked into the trap of Shrailzhar. The remembering of it tumbled in her belly and she felt ill.

"Take it," he said. As he did, he held it up for Jennifer to stick her arms through. "I'm sorry I didn't offer it to you sooner," he sighed. "I never even thought the extra weight would help you to stay on the ground."

And there it was—the answer she had asked Simeon for. Of course! The cloak would not make her an easier target; it would make her a heavier one!

Jennifer stuffed her arms into the holes and wrapped it around herself. Matt was much bigger than Jennifer, yet, she was not surprised when his cloak fit her perfectly. Not much in the strange land of Trilleah surprised her ... not anymore.

"Let's go," she squealed, and out they went. She pulled her hands inside and felt something in one of the pockets. As her fingers went along the sides of something, feeling careful, she realized what it was; the clay tablets. She wished she'd put on a different cloak because suddenly the responsibility of the one she was tucked into seemed too great.

She didn't want to cause any more of a stir, nor take any more of their time, so she hushed and said nothing—although now it felt heavy on her shoulders and heavy in her soul.

The Travelers—some with cloaks and some without—huddled together. They held on to one another because it was the only way they would not get tossed about by the winds. Those hard, roaring winds were circling now, picking up larger boulders and hurling them across the land—as though they were nothing more than tiny pebbles.

A loud wail screeched through the air and the Travelers knew the Leviathan had finally lost his battle with the lightning. There was such a great divide in the sky now, and from somewhere up above there were the tiniest shreds of light beginning to poke through.

They looked like stars, but not shining stars like one might imagine in the heavenlies. They were more like stars that had been lassoed in and pulled to a place where they were forbidden to twinkle. Maybe they were not stars at all. Judah noticed them first and wondered about them; they all saw him looking up and followed his gaze. The sky opened up much wider now, and those things he was noticing began to hurl themselves down upon him and the others.

They looked small from above the torn sky, but as they were hurled to the ground with great fury, the Travelers saw they were indeed very large. Monstrous even! Judah and the others weaved and ducked and tried their best to stay out of the way of the smoldering boulders. They were coming down hard around them on every side, making the land shake even more. It seemed, at first, like they were being launched straight at the Travelers, but as they worked to avoid being taken out by the closest ones, the Travelers realized they were being hurled down everywhere—all over the land.

Oh, there were so many of those giant balls of black rock catapulting down, surely the ground could not take the pummeling and would give way. Whatever might be underneath—if anything at all—the Travelers feared they might soon find out. Jennifer's mind flashed back to another journey on another solstice where she'd seen something peer out from beneath the ground, when Sam had been dragging a large branch and, though he didn't know it, was opening the ground. She shuttered.

"JUDAH," Jennifer shouted. Even though her lips were right next to her brother's ear, she wondered if her voice reached him. "I'M SO AFRAID!" He grabbed her arm and squeezed tightly. He wanted to answer her with a loud "me too," but knew his sister needed him to be brave for her, and so, he was.

"NUTTIN TO BE SCARED ABOUT, JELLY BEAN," he shouted instead. "NUTTIN AT ALL!"

That was enough for Jennifer to keep going. She knew her brother was lying and that was okay with her; she knew it was only because he loved her. He wasn't trying to fool her or make her believe something that wasn't so; he was trying to give her courage.

And he did.

Jennifer took a deep breath even though the air was thick and smelled like sulfur. As they pushed against the winds and tried with all their might to keep moving forward—even though they would get pushed back often—she let the breath fill her up with peace. She finally let it seep through her teeth and like air being let out of a balloon, a squeal escaped her lips.

Judah looked over at her and let out a laugh, which was contagious and sent her on a roll of laughter as well. The others looked at the twins and had no idea what could be funny right about now. It wasn't anything that was funny, really, just that awkward chuckle that comes from being in an unpredictable predicament.

It was a good thing the twins' had caught the other's attention; as the Travelers looked back at the twins, they saw that the massive boulders that had been hurling themselves down from beyond the sky were beginning to ignite into flame.

"LOOK," Sam shrieked. They looked.

KABOOM

Trilleah shook hard as three of the flaming boulders smashed into the ground. The land shook hard, and the Travelers wobbled. Some fell to their knees but the ones who remained standing pulled them right back up and kept on going—a little faster.

"We can't stop," Pierce hollered.

This shaking and tripping and stumbling went on and on. The flaming boulders smashed into the ground, causing the land to shake, which made the Travelers teeter and wobble. Jennifer's feet were bleeding—terribly cut and blistered. Oh, how she wished for those boots that she'd thought so ugly before. If only she could have them back on her feet now, she'd never complain about them again.

But that was not to be; her boots had been hit by one of the flaming boulders that were being thrown from the sky and had burned up. In fact, if they could see the spot where Pierce and Jennifer had sat on the shore of the sea only a few hours earlier, they'd have been horrified to find the shore—all of it—gone.

With all of the lightning that had pierced Leviathan and the hundreds of flaming boulders that had already been hurled from somewhere above Trilleah's sky, the shore had been dissolved. The sea had pushed its way up and had swallowed the shore completely. Not one grain of sand or morsel of crud or shred of evidence that there ever was a shore, remained.

It had all been destroyed, along with Jennifer's boots and the left-behind cloaks.

An unfamiliar voice came to the Travelers and echoed back and forth between them. One looked at another who looked over toward someone else. Each wanted to see who had spoken the words. Whichever of the Travelers had said them, the others would have to shut them up. There was no room for such fearful thoughts here!

"It is certainly too late for you," the voice sneered. "Not one of you will return to your pathetic hollow. It's been destroyed, and you will be destroyed as well."

The Travelers' eyes were all as big as the moon, looking from one to the next, trying to find the owner of such deplorable words.

Who would say such a thing? Bella wondered.

But indeed, it was not a "who" that had spoken the terrible words at all … it was a what. And that "what" now hovered among them.

Missing Maps

3

"What?" Bella demanded. "Who said such a thing?"

"YA," Pierce ordered looking around. "Who said that?"

One by one, amidst the howling winds, the rumbling ground, and the torn-open sky, the Travelers swore it was not any of their tongues that had uttered the ugly words. Their eyes were opened large, looking around the group. There was no doubt that an unwelcome trespasser had joined them. None of them saw anybody who wasn't supposed to be there, but it wasn't long before a dull red murk settled among them.

It was nothing like the mist that had been in the land yesterday—the one that had hovered around Leviathan and had tried to hide him. This one wasn't as thick and was most definitely red.

"I said it," came a sneer from the murk.

Now, the Travelers had not seen anything such as this before, and while some wanted to run, others wanted to stop.

"It is I who am telling you these things," the voice sneered again. "You will get no farther than you are this very minute."

It's a strange thing when there are words but no tongue to form them. It's a stranger thing still when the words are not heard by the ears, but by the soul. And the souls of every Traveler heard the words coming from out of the red murk. The more words uttered, the more paralyzed in fear the Travelers became. Inside of their minds, the Shailmas were each instructing their riders to *Say this*, or *Holler that*, but the minds of the Travelers were stuck. They wanted to shout the words their Shailmas were feeding them. Some of them tried and failed—time after time—some never tried at all.

They couldn't open their mouths, and so they remained hushed, silently watching the red murk hover as it twisted this way and that between this Traveler and over that one. It was so close to their skin yet not close enough to touch them. It weaved and twisted; twisted and weaved.

All of a sudden their mouths were unlatched and they did let out a yell … and a hoot … and a holler …

There, right in front of them, was Asphelia's Hollow. Bella reached her foot out and stuck it nervously into the small opening at the bottom of the rock covering the entrance. When she did, it opened wide and the dull red murk that had been taunting them for the last few minutes scurried away, rocketing up into the sky and dissolving—disappearing altogether—into the atmosphere.

Bella tumbled into the hollow first, and then Jennifer and Judah, followed by Pierce, Kaija Mae, and the others. Laying inside their hollow all jumbled in one big pile, they began laughing. They laid there nervously laughing so hard and for so long until finally their bellies hurt and demanded they stop. They tried, oh how they tried, but the overwhelming relief of being safely inside Asphelia's Hollow was so great that laughing was all they could do, and it felt good.

Now, there is never a good time for laughing in a land such as Trilleah, but sometimes, laughing is all one can do. Fear has a way of standing back when so much laughter is being done. Finally grabbing their bellies while wheezing and gasping for breath, they tired themselves right out, and the laughing wafted off to be looked for later.

After laying on the floor a few more minutes and catching their breath, they began putting their feet under them and standing up; one by one. First Jennifer, and then Judah, and then Kaija Mae.

Jennifer looked around, and it seemed for the most part that the hollow had not been shaken or touched or upset whatsoever. Sure, there were mites of dust here that had been blown around and over there a small pile of stones which had shaken loose, but the ceiling was above them and the floor was beneath them. What more could they ask for?

The Travelers rejoiced and jumped and hollered and danced. They were sure that if they ever found Asphelia's Hollow, it would be shaken to bits. It's nice, sometimes, to be so very wrong. This was one of those times.

"Unfortunately, we have no time to wander through the hollow," Bella said. She was back to her bossy self, and even though nobody enjoyed that side of her, it was necessary, and so right now, nobody particularly minded. Pierce spoke up without waiting for Bella to give him his usual orders.

"I'll find the maps." He hurried to the basket where the maps were usually kept, but instead of hearing any happy words, the others heard deep gasps pouring from him.

"What is it?" Judah asked. He moved toward the basket to see what Pierce was going on about. Judah hoped to find nothing out of the ordinary, but this was one of the times when being wrong was not good. Not good at all! Before Judah could get close to the basket of maps, Pierce had picked it up and tipped it upside down over his head. "They're gone," he sighed.

It bewildered some, where the maps would go. If the hollow had been disheveled or if the winds had somehow gotten in and blown them out of the basket or the roof had fallen in, it would have made sense. But none of that had happened. It did not bewilder others. Not even slightly.

"Pierce," Jennifer said. "We left Miriam in the hollow alone. We should have known she'd destroy whatever she could!"

"Oh no!" Pierce screeched. "I cannot believe her!" That was all he said; even though she had been thrown into the sea by Leviathan, Miriam was, after all, his cousin. No matter what she'd done or how wretched she had become or what blood covenants she'd made with the king, Pierce still felt deeply saddened and responsible for her demise.

But for now, those feelings were overshadowed by anger. For now, they had no maps. Bella jumped, startling those around her and started to run toward the passageway leading to the kitchen. "I hope that wretched little … she began to rant about what she thought of Miriam but then remembered that Pierce was her cousin and so she stopped herself. "I hope she left the food," was all she said. Sam and Kaija Mae and a few others followed Bella and soon they were out of sight.

Jennifer was curious about the food as well, and about what might be missing from her own Sleeping Chamber. But as deep as her curiosity was, her sadness for Pierce was deeper. She stayed back to try and be whatever help she could be for the young man she'd only yesterday loathed and wished ill upon.

Pierce wiped the bottom of the empty basket for no reason, but he didn't know what else to do. His job had always been to dig around in the maps and find the ones they had needed. Now, with no maps to dig through, he was lost and felt without purpose for the next journey which was about to begin at any moment.

He was overcome with emotion, and the angry feelings won out for the time being. Pierce threw the basket against the wall and watched it smash into smithereens. That was not enough to appease his anger, and he took a step and kicked it, breaking it even more.

Jennifer and Judah took a few steps toward him. They wanted to tell Pierce that his anger wasn't going to help. They both wanted to calm him down, but Matt stepped in front of the twins and cut them off.

"Just let him be," Matt whispered. "He needs to get it out."

"Okay," Jennifer said. Judah nodded. They both headed in different directions and Pierce fell back against the wall. He slid down until he was sitting on the floor among the pieces of the broken basket.

Yes, Jennifer thought to herself. *I better leave him alone.*

She headed toward the passageway that would lead her to the kitchen but stopped and turned back. She went to Pierce and took his hand. He pulled it away, but she grabbed it again, not easily put off.

"Jen," Matt said.

"It's okay, Matt," she replied. "I've got this." And indeed, she did have it. Simeon had put a thought in her head, and when Simeon gave Jennifer a thought, she listened. Nothing was able to stop her from following the directions of her Shailma; not even Pierce.

"Come," she said firmly to Pierce and pulled on his arm. Now, two days ago, or even yesterday, Pierce would have ripped his hand away and told Jennifer to … well, he would have muttered something terribly rude to her, no doubt.

But not today.

Something had changed between the two unlikely Travelers, and as Matt and Judah took a step back, they could see the change and knew better than to interfere with whatever was happening. It was bigger than either of them, so they watched with anticipation as two of the most unlikely Travelers disappeared—hand in hand—into the dim passageway.

Matt wondered where they were headed, but Judah knew. He knew because, on the last journey, that dreadful day when the earth had swallowed up Jennifer, and Judah had been overcome with despair, Pierce had done the same thing to him that he just watched Jennifer do with Pierce.

"She's taking him to the Chamber of Rest," Judah said.

"Ah, a great idea," Matt replied. "Should we go with them?"

Judah thought for a minute but then decided against it. "I wonder if just those two need to be in the chamber for a time," he said. Matt agreed and so the two boys headed to the kitchen where they hoped to find some food.

As soon as Jennifer grabbed Pierce by the hand and pulled him to his feet, the young man knew exactly where she was taking him. They darted through where the entrance was, with Jennifer leading him all the way to the bench that was still tucked into the dimness.

She reached down and lifted the lid. The secret chamber opened itself up to the two weary Travelers, and they stepped inside. Jennifer didn't have to coax Pierce even a little; he stepped in immediately.

He remembered back to their last journey when he had to persuade Judah to step inside after the boys had thought they'd lost Jennifer—the very one who now brought him.

How crazy is that? Pierce thought to himself as he stuck a note in his memory to tell Jennifer about it later.

For now, he soaked up all the rest he could open himself up to.

Jennifer was busy wondering what would happen to all this peace and beauty and wonder if the hollow were to be destroyed. Surely it would not be able to stand alone if Trilleah were to succeed in self-destructing. It was a thought much too sad for Jennifer to embrace and she let it go.

This is not the time for such wonderings, Jenny, she heard Simeon whisper to her mind. *This is the time to soak up as much peace and beauty and wonder as you can, for a time is coming when this chamber will be no more. But you, my Little One, you will need all you can take with you—a full measure—from this place.*

How can I take anything from here? she wondered of her Shailma. Her eyes darted this way and that, looking for something— anything—she might be able to take with her. She found nothing, which was exactly what she expected to find.

A Full Measure

4

Jenny, Simeon scolded teasingly, *I do not mean to take those things that you can put in your pocket or hold in your hand.* Simeon was always so kind, but sometimes he must have wondered how this one—this Jennifer who was so simple-minded and genuinely naive—had been called to be the Curse Breaker.

Well, what am I supposed to take then, Simeon? She was puzzled. Truly she thought he'd meant she was supposed to take a piece of the crimson rock that was so beautiful. Or maybe a stone from the emerald wall or a small chip from the crystal floor.

If none of these were the things she was supposed to take, then she was bewildered since she saw nothing else. Jennifer strained her eyes to see into the corners of the room but found nothing there either. It wasn't hard to see into every nook and cranny in this chamber because there wasn't a shadow to be seen anywhere. Jennifer decided to look for a shadow and spent a good amount of time searching. She found none.

The light which seemed to come from nowhere—a source all its own—glistened off every bump and crack. Jennifer ran her socked foot along the floor hoping for a piece of the crystal that had broken off but found nothing. The floor was as smooth as glass, without even a piece of lint or a bit of wayward dirt scattered on it.

It had a fire set within it, but there was no heat being sent out and it was not burning up. Jennifer didn't recall there being a fire burning in the crystal floor the last time she was in this chamber, but perhaps she'd just forgotten. She had seen a lot since her last time in the Chamber of Rest and maybe her mind was confused or forgetful of such things.

Finally, after Simeon had been thoroughly amused by Jennifer's lighthearted but focused search for something—anything—to take with her, he came again to her mind.

No, Jenny. You are to take all you can squeeze into your heart, Little One, her Shailma instructed. *Breathe deeply,* he advised. *I've enlarged your heart's capacity for such a time as this.*

Now she felt embarrassed; she should have known that was what he meant. Simeon calmed her, though, and her embarrassment was soon replaced with peace and wonder and rest—and deep breaths. Many, many deep breaths. Inhaling such a pure air filled her heart. It felt like a tall glass of cold water on a hot, hot day; completely refreshing, utterly soothing, altogether wonderful. She tried to breathe even deeper.

Yes, this was precisely what her Shailma meant. Jennifer looked over at Pierce who was lying against the far wall. He was breathing through his nose and blowing the breaths out peacefully through his mouth. Jennifer knew he, too, was filling up on all that was available in this chamber. She laid back, closed her eyes, and did the same.

Oh, the refreshing washing of one's heart that took place here in this space. Such deep rest filled them both. Inhaling so much peace forced out all that was not peaceful. There was no more room for anger toward Miriam or sadness that the sea had swallowed her up or fear of what might yet come to be.

The shaking of Trilleah seemed to be unable to shake this room, for it was perfectly still and altogether calm. There was no way Jennifer could know that all of Trilleah had momentarily stopped shaking because the king had arranged for his army to take prisoner all of the Travelers. It was only a matter of time, though, before she would find out. When she did, oh how she would beg Simeon to bring her back to the Chamber of Rest.

"I should go get the others," she finally whispered to Pierce.

"They'll come," he replied without opening his eyes or moving a muscle. "They will come."

And they did come. No sooner had the words slipped from his mouth than the secret entrance behind the deep blue wall slid open to welcome Judah, Matt, and Kaija Mae. The three of them said nothing but nodded toward Jennifer who watched them enter. They each found a place on the floor, or in a corner or against a wall, and sat or laid down or sprawled themselves out.

There was only one thing to do here, and that was to breathe deeply and fill up on all the chamber offered. It didn't seem like much, and to explain to someone else how wonderful it was to be in this chamber—well—they would not have understood.

It was an easy task, though, to breathe deeply, for the very beauty of the chamber washed over any ugliness that was hovering or hidden in the Travelers' minds. Whatever fear, dread, or anger one of them entered with, those things would be left behind for the chamber to dispose of.

Oh, the pure and complete rest that wrapped itself around their outsides and fluttered throughout their insides. It sometimes felt like their bones just melted away inside this chamber, making it hard to stay upright—which is probably why everyone leaned against a wall or laid on the floor. It was just easiest that way.

Now, one might think just being *in* the Chamber of Rest was utterly amazing and oh, it was. But if there was anything in the whole world that could make it even better—more peaceful—it was Kaija

Mae's singing. When she began singing her sweet melodies now, quietly and to herself, all the beautiful things offered in the chamber were that much better; sweeter somehow.

Jennifer looked up, since her eyes had been closed, and thought for a moment that she could actually see the chamber filling with a sweet scent that rode on the wings of the songs.

Truly, there was nothing better, not in this land or any other.

Jennifer glanced toward Pierce, and when she saw the spot where he'd been laying was empty, she sprang up to a sitting position. *Where did he go?* she wondered. Jennifer looked over to where the others had been and saw only she and Kaija Mae remained in the chamber.

Jennifer jumped to her feet, although still very full of peace, and asked Kaija Mae if she'd seen the others leave.

"I did," the girl said with a smile.

"Where did they go?" Jennifer asked. She wondered whether she should feel some panic but immediately felt so washed with the fragrance of the Chamber of Rest that no panic came; there was no room for it—only simple curiosity.

Oh, how she wished this feeling could be with her always. How wonderful it would be to carry this with her everywhere she went —just like Simeon had said.

"Out," was all that Kaija Mae finally said in response to Jennifer's question.

"We should go too, then," Jennifer said. She closed her eyes and breathed in deeply one more time. She held it for as long as she could before letting it seep its way out of her lungs.

"I suppose the time has come," Kaija Mae replied and did the same as Jennifer.

With one last glance back inside the chamber, the girls stepped out and the secret entrance closed itself up. That was that. They both knew—or supposed, anyway—they would not be back inside the Chamber of Rest again. They lingered for few minutes longer, letting the memories of the most magnificent of all places find somewhere to hide inside their memories.

"It's about time you two came out of there," they heard Pierce say.

"We didn't even know you left," Jennifer answered. "Well, I didn't know anyway. What was your hurry?"

"Hurry?" Judah asked. "Jen, you were in there for well over an hour!" he responded.

"Oh," was all she could think of to say since she really couldn't believe it was that long. *He's exaggerating,* she thought but didn't say so just in case he wasn't.

Time in the Chamber of Rest could zoom by so quickly yet it seemed to those inside, that stood still.

"We were just coming to get you," Matt said. "There's no more time—we have to go!"

But Jennifer's stomach was rumbling something horrible, reminding her how very hungry she was. It seemed in Trilleah, she was hungry much of the time and said so now.

"Did Bella find any food?" she asked. "Or did Miriam take that, too?"

"There was a little, yes," Judah said. "Bella's already packed it all up, and we're ready to go."

"Where are we going without a map?" Kaija Mae asked now since it seemed foolish to venture into Trilleah without one. There would be no indication of where to go, or where the army was marching, or what creatures might be waiting for them where, or if the king was out and about searching for them. "It seems fallacious to try and find a tablet without any maps," she concluded.

"How do we even know what direction to go?" Jennifer asked. She chuckled but did not find the situation funny. Sometimes she just laughed in frustrating or uncomfortable situations. This was definitely both frustrating and uncomfortable, but certainly not funny.

Pierce must have known what the others were thinking because without being asked, he replied. He was so much kinder now, since yesterday, but there still seemed to be something unpredictable about him; something was just a bit off; mysterious even. Jennifer decided to put it out of her mind for now.

"We have no other options," he mumbled. "We either go without a map or we don't go." Everyone was thinking the same thing, more or less. But there was much to consider and no time to consider it.

"If King Shrailzhar is out, I doubt he'll be looking for us," Judah offered. "He's set on destroying the land before we can find the last tablet. I think he'll probably not even bother with us now."

"He's probably already gone," Kaija Mae offered. "If he's intent on destroying the land, and it seems he is, I would think he'd want to be gone long before his kingdom falls into destruction!" She didn't know for certain if this was true or not, but Kaija Mae—and the others—hoped it was.

Not the Little One

5

Some agreed with Kaija Mae and Judah, and some did not, but there was one thing they all agreed on; the fact that they had no other option. The sands of time had nearly all run through the hourglass, and the land was intent on self-destruction.

They had to go, and they had to go now.

"Either we find the last tablet, break the curse, and release the souls or we don't and the souls remain cursed for eternity," Matt said. "Are we going to give up now?" he asked.

"Well, when you put it that way," Jennifer whined, "I suppose not."

"Then let's get going!" Pierce said with a hint of peculiarness in his voice.

The Travelers should have been far more cautious and thought through their decision much more carefully. While they believed the king was no longer searching for them, that was not the truth. They believed such foolishness because, well, because they wanted to believe it. If any one of them had asked their Shailmas for wisdom or even thought about it slightly, they would have known differently.

The king, of course, was not willing to lose even one of the souls that his Trows had stolen. That foolish king still hoped he could keep both the souls and his kingdom. He wondered, though, when weakness would set into his bones, if he may have to give up one or the other. Only time would tell—time always does.

It seemed everyone in Trilleah believed lies of all sorts of varieties and sizes, and all were believing the most unbelievable things. The question had become whose wrong beliefs would cost them the most? The king's? Or the Travelers'?

Now it must be said that the Travelers were all thankful that Asphelia's Hollow had once again miraculously provided everyone with cloaks … The hollow almost always provided what had been lost, or misplaced, or broken. It was just the way it was with the hollow. Nobody could explain it, or even understand it, and it didn't take long before everyone quit trying to do either and was simply thankful. There were many things in Trilleah that had no explanation, and this was just one of those many things.

Once each Traveler was safely tucked inside their cloaks and hidden within the hoods, they were ready to go. Bella had the food—what was left of it—stashed inside of her cloak, and there was nothing else to take. The maps were gone and they had no idea what else they may need, so they took nothing—nothing that is, except for the little green jar that Jennifer had secretly tucked inside her pocket. She didn't know why, but she thought it might come in handy at some point and really, it was very tiny, so it was better to have it and not need it than to need it and not have it.

Finally ready, one by one, they stepped back out into Trilleah. The Travelers were surprised, but then again not so much, when they saw the Dark Land no longer looked anything like it did only a few hours before—when they had tumbled into the hollow. They wouldn't have recognized it at all if they didn't already know what land it was. It looked like a giant had picked up their little hollow and dropped it somewhere they'd never been before. It looked even more dead than before—if such a thing were possible. It had no life at all; even the air had a smell to it that was unsettling and unfamiliar.

"Uh, where did the trees go?" Jennifer asked. She sounded horrified because, well, she was! Nobody heard her, though. The words didn't get out of her hood, so she screamed. "WHERE IS THE FOREST? WHERE'S .... MY ... MAMMA?"

The forest had obviously been moved, and now the only thing they could see for a very long distance was the one large boulder that covered their hollow. Besides that, much of the land was burned up and the ground was filled with singed craters—from the fireballs that the sky had hurled down—they supposed.

Jennifer was shocked that she seemed to be the only one who was terrified that the forest was no longer where their eyes could see it. She didn't know if it had been moved somewhere else in Trilleah, or if it had been destroyed altogether. Maybe it had been burned up in whatever had singed the ground. She couldn't breathe. Fear ripped through her and squeezed her heart mercilessly. Her mamma's soul was in that forest. As Jennifer tried to imagine where the forest may have gone, her breath began to speed up, making it hard for her not to choke.

Breathe, Jennifer. Breathe, she heard Simeon command firmly. *This is why you needed to fill up your entire being in the Chamber of Rest. This is why I informed you then—because you need all of that peace and rest and comfort NOW.*

Jennifer looked at Bella and then toward Matt, and finally to Judah. She was looking for the same fear that had erupted in her, hoping to find it in someone else's eyes so she didn't feel so alone in her pain. She didn't, and she didn't understand why.

They must have heard their Shailmas already, she thought.

Jennifer let the words of Simeon run through her mind again and again until they were firm in her heart. She determined to follow his instruction and tried with all her might to go back into the storage of her mind to find what she had tucked away there earlier, from the

Chamber of Rest. She was able to find bits and pieces, though barely enough to calm her, but enough to keep going.

"There's another one," Judah said and pointed to a boulder. That one looked very similar to the one they'd just come out of, only smaller.

"There's another one over there!" shouted Sam and sure enough, there was. Soon their eyes were seeing boulders dotting the flat, now treeless area. Some were enormous—way bigger than the one covering their hollow—and some were small enough to miss entirely if they weren't looking carefully. With Malleana Forest out of the way, it made all the boulders easy to spot.

"Are they all hollows?" Bella asked. She didn't expect an answer, it was more of a general wondering than an actual question, but she got one nevertheless.

"Yes," Kaija Mae responded. "They are." She pointed to one that was way over to the left, nearly out of sight. "That was our hollow," she said and sounded disappointed they hadn't been there in a long while. She spent a bit of time describing her own hollow and where the chambers were and how the Eating Chamber was different than Asphelia's.

"What?" Judah sputtered.

"There are that many hollows?" Jennifer shrieked.

"Shh!" Bella hushed them all. "Keep your voices down," she scolded. They didn't know what—or who—may be near, watching or listening. "We need to whisper!" Bella commanded. They knew there were no Trows here since Trows could only live in the trees—when they weren't skulking around stealing souls, that is.

Kaija Mae lowered her voice and tried to explain a few more things before the others could ask a hundred questions. "The land is filled with hollows because the land was never meant to be the way it is now," she began. She looked around at the Travelers and saw they all had the same confused looks smeared across their faces, so she continued; before she did, she made a suggestion.

"We should probably not stand here in the open like this," she said. "We need to pick a direction and then go that way!" The Travelers looked around, wondering which way to go. Confusion was everywhere, but a path could not be found anywhere. How were they supposed to just "pick a direction" in such an upside-down land?

It was a precarious predicament that the Travelers were not being cautious or hiding. Since they had no maps to show them where the enemy was or where the army was marching or where King Shrailzhar may be hiding, most dangers were not in the front of their minds.

"Any suggestions?" Kaija Mae finally asked since it was clear nobody was going to offer any.

Pierce spoke up. "Let's think for a minute here before we just go willy-nilly wandering one way or another." They thought, and they discussed, and they tried to remember which way they went for each of the tablets. They had no need to get to the Carphlour Caves to read the maps since they didn't have any maps to read.

All this wondering and figuring proved harder than they had thought, though, because the Dark Land had turned itself so far around and inside out and upside down that they couldn't tell the east from the west or the north from the south. They just stood in a clump out in the openness of the land, dumbfounded. While they felt hidden inside their cloaks, they were certainly not hidden … and they MOST certainly were not alone.

"Oh dear," Bella sighed, as she always did when overwhelming confusion strained her mind.

Pierce noticed Matt, who was moving toward Bella, and he quickly threw his arm around her before Matt could reach her.

"Don't worry, Bella, we'll figure it out," he said sweetly. Too sweetly. Jennifer wanted to roll her eyes, but since there was nobody who'd notice, she didn't bother.

Matt moved closer to Bella even though Pierce was clearly trying to send him a signal. Matt ignored it and stepped right in front of her.

"Bella," he said, "we'll get to where we need to go, wherever that might be."

They looked this way … and they looked that way. They hummed … and they hawed. They looked up above … and they looked down below. Finally, Jennifer spoke up. The entire time everyone else was trying to figure things out on their own, she had been discussing with Simeon the right way to go.

"It's this way," she huffed impatiently and finally rolled her eyes at the boys who seemed much more interested in Bella than in finding the last tablet. Jennifer began marching—bootless, but at least back in her old sneakers—toward the very direction they'd just returned from earlier this morning. She was not concerned whether anyone would follow her or not. It seemed they were all waiting for someone to step up and make a decision. They followed her without even one of the Travelers asking her "Who do you think you are," or "Why should we follow you," or even, "What makes you think you know the right way to go?" Everyone seemed to be relieved that someone other than them had made a decision.

"Now," Kaija Mae stated. "Let me tell you about the hollows."

So, for the next long while, as Jennifer trudged along jumping over cracks and crevasses in the ground that the Dark Land had shaken open, and weaving this way and that as Simeon directed her, everyone else followed closely behind. At the same time, Kaija Mae told the Travelers all about the land of Trilleah—at least, all she knew of the Dark Land—long before they had all come to it.

They listened carefully, utterly amazed by all she said because truly, the only ones to know that Kaija Mae had been here for such a long time were the few others who'd had their own souls wrongly taken, such as Aviel and Tahlia—and the one to whom she had already revealed her secret—Judah. Even Jennifer had no idea she was so very old and had been here from the beginning of Trilleah.

"And I suppose it must have been the Shailmas who led you to that hollow when you first came to Trilleah, Bella. There is no other way you would have found it," said Kaija Mae.

"I don't understand," Bella answered.

"Have you never wondered how you came upon your hollow and we come upon ours?" Kaija Mae asked. "Or how the king was unable to find any of the hollows if it was his land that had made them? I have wondered," she hesitated. "I've wondered many times if it was the Shailmas who put the hollows in Trilleah for us. I always assumed the king put the boulders in the land, but the Shailmas must have put the hollows beneath them."

So much information to consider and so many deep things to wonder about was confusing to everyone. While Kaija Mae had *many* of the answers—for indeed she was here from the beginning—she did not have *all* the answers. Not even close to all the answers. She had not even thought of all the questions!

"All I know," she said, "was when those of us who had been wrongly taken by the Trows could not be held under the curse, we needed somewhere to be. We couldn't go back home, and we couldn't stay out here in the land." When she said that last part, she waved her hands around wildly to remind the others exactly where "out here" was.

"I suppose not," Judah replied. He found the girl very mysterious and she was beautiful by anyone's standards. He had to keep reminding himself that she was very old, even though he didn't recall how old, and she was not at all how his eyes saw her. It was hard for his mind—or anyone's mind for that matter—to remember she was an old lady since she did not look old or act old.

"How did you know so many things then?" Sam asked. "Even if you were here from the beginning, that wouldn't necessarily mean you know everything about it."

"The same way any of you did, of course," she answered with a giggle. "I also have a Shailma, and he was able to lead me and tell me where to go and how to dwell here in this undwellable land."

"I suppose," Sam muttered since he'd never considered such a thing.

The Travelers talked too long, and they allowed their conversation to capture their attention too deeply. They failed to notice what had come up behind them. It was a good distance behind them, but all the Army of Shrailzhar was behind them nonetheless.

This was the very reason Malleana Forest had been moved. Trilleah had shaken the land ferociously hard until every tree from the forest had been uprooted and blown. The roots were not deep since the trees were not really trees, of course, and they had no need for their roots to go deep. Furthermore, there was nothing deep beneath the ground for the roots to weave down into.

The king knew the Travelers would be heading back to their beloved Asphelia's Hollow, but he also knew there were far too many of those dreadful hollows to find any particular one anymore— specifically, the one to which those dreadful Curse Breakers kept returning. They'd found it once, but with such shaking and changes to the land, the chances of the army finding it a second time were unlikely.

So, the king had forged a plan—together with the Dark Land and his army—and together, they would find the Curse Breakers' hollow.

To the land, he ordered, "Shake and tremble and quiver until the trees come loose and give way from your ground."

To the wind, he commanded, "Gather all your winds together and blast and roar and blow until you pick up every last tree in Malleana Forest. Carry them across the land to the far side, the other side of the sea and drop them into the Chasm of Acheron."

To his army, he instructed, "Hide beyond the horizon, where those wretched Curse Breakers will not see you. When they leave whichever hollow it is that has betrayed me by hiding them, follow them. Demolish the hollow thoroughly first of all, and when that has been completed, destroy them—those dreadful Travelers. How dare they think they could come into MY land and take back what now belongs to ME!"

The king thought about this final instruction for a moment and then came back and said to the Chief of his army, "But when you destroy them, whistle for the Trows to come so they can steal those wretched mortals' miserable souls. I want every single one of their odious and vile souls to be chained and under my curse for all of eternity."

And then, that deplorable king added one more command. Shrailzhar raised his voice loudly and shrieked, "DESTROY EVERY LAST ONE OF THEM, EXCEPT FOR THAT WICKED LITTLE GIRL … That one, I will snuff out myself." He laughed a most hideous laugh, for the thought of finally capturing Jennifer's soul and cursing it to his forest made him crazy with excitement.

That despicable, detestable, lowdown and completely awful king rubbed his hands together as if he was about to devour a most wonderfully delightful meal. Perhaps he felt like he was!

The Dark Land fearfully obeyed the king's commands and had done exactly as he'd set for them to do. The winds blew violently this way and that and had carried the trees over the sea and piled them just beyond the Chasm of Acheron. Now it was up to his army to carry out the final phase of his plan. Oh, how his excitement was growing and burning within him.

The Army of Shrailzhar would do its best to make sure the souls of all those who had caused so much disturbance to the king—and so much havoc to Trilleah—would quickly be trapped under the dreadful curse of the Trows for all of time.

The king would have charge of his kingdom once again.

In Clear View

6

The Travelers were completely unaware of the Army of Shrailzhar that was coming up behind them, although they'd been wondering why the land was so quiet. Without Malleana Forest there with all its painful groaning and wretched moaning, it was much too quiet.

Eerily quiet …

Ghostly quiet …

Painfully quiet …

It made the hairs on the back of their necks stand on end and their mouths go dry. Suddenly, each Traveler realized how painful such a quiet could be. It poked through their skin and carved worry into their bones.

The Travelers had not yet realized the movements of the army. They didn't realize the land was hushed because it was fearfully watching Shrailzhar's Army. The land held its breath. Trilleah knew if the armies were unable to overtake the Travelers, if they failed in their one quest, then the land was to self-destruct immediately—or, as soon as possible. Destroying an entire land might take a bit of time, after all.

Yes, Trilleah watched painstakingly carefully, every movement of the army.

It was tricky for Jennifer, trying to follow a path where there wasn't one. Nonetheless, Simeon faithfully kept leading her, and she was very busy listening to him, looking intently with the eyes of her heart. But, she was also becoming more and more distracted by Kaija Mae's stories and constant chattering.

For a time, Jennifer forgot to listen at all to the only one she should have been listening to all along. She ended up wandering ahead without waiting to hear a direction, although the others assumed Simeon was still leading her. As is usually the case with assuming, the Travelers were wrong. Irreparably wrong.

BOOM!!!!

Jennifer was listening now! Something had shaken Trilleah considerably and demanded her full attention straightaway.

The land was not shaking the same as before, where the ground vibrated with tremors, and it was hard to stand for long. This shaking was one big blast. One gigantic push. As though the entire Dark Land had been hurled through the air and stopped suddenly, hitting something perhaps.

The Travelers were violently hurled to the ground and they covered their heads; it was indeed a thunderous ruckus. For a time, they stayed down—hidden beneath their cloaks—and determined to remain motionless. They were not sure if there was another blast coming, so they waited … just in case.

After a time, nothing else was heard so slowly, cautiously, they stood back up to their feet.

SIMEON! Jennifer hollered in her mind. *WHAT WAS THAT?* she demanded to know.

Little One, it was the Shailmas, was the calm answer that came to her mind.

WHAT? She must have heard wrong. Surely the Shailmas would not cause such an enormous crash of Trilleah! Certainly, they would not purposely hurl the Travelers to the ground like that, would they? Yes, she must have heard wrong.

Jennifer, Simeon said at seeing her doubting mind, *you did not hear me wrong. None of the Travelers are paying attention to their Shailmas, and you were not paying attention to me. It's of utmost importance that you do,* he scolded.

Whatever we must do to get your attention in a time of such important matters, we will do. You have become so distracted by what HAS HAPPENED that you are not noticing what IS HAPPENING right now. Don't look back to the past, nor ahead to the future. Stay focused on the present—that's where your thoughts must remain. None of you has even realized the Army of Shrailzhar is coming up behind you and in fact, are about to seize you all! Simeon continued his scolding.

Jennifer didn't know what to say. It was true that she had lost focus and had stopped listening to Simeon and had started listening to Kaija Mae instead. Her mind whizzed with all that Simeon had just told her.

You let yourself become too distracted and now you and the others are in grave danger. The Shailmas had to come together and shake Trilleah to get your attention.

Jennifer did not want to turn around or tell the others what Simeon had told her. She didn't need to since their own Shailmas had scolded them as well.

"Judah," Jennifer called quietly.

"I'm here," was all he replied.

"The army is behind us," she whispered and crossed her fingers because she did not want to alarm anyone, yet she was so very alarmed herself.

"I know," he said. "Shemaiah told me."

"Shura told me as well," Bella whispered.

"Mishan told me, too," Matt added. One by one, the Travelers mentioned how their Shailmas had warned them about the dangers lurking behind. Everyone had a quiver in their voices, so Jennifer knew she was not the only one who was full of terror.

"What do we do?" she whimpered. They had merely kept on walking so far, although they'd picked up their pace significantly, as though walking faster might allow them to escape Shrailzhar's Army. None wanted to turn behind to see, so for now, none did. For now, they kept their eyes wide open and looking straight ahead.

"I don't know," Bella said. She sounded like she was near tears, but there was no time for that in Jennifer's mind.

Simeon, she begged, *what do we do? I am truly sorry I let Kaija Mae's stories become more important than your directions. Simeon, I'm so sorry!* she anguished deep in her heart.

The words that came back to her mind brought instant comfort because she had experienced before exactly what he was explaining to her now. The others, however, wouldn't be so sure and Jennifer had to keep them from panicking and becoming completely undone and useless.

Little One, she heard from Simeon, who was no longer scolding her, *I have summoned for all the Shamar Warriors to come together. They are arriving even now. I will open your eyes to see, but only for a moment—like in the adder's pit.*

Look around you, Jenny, she heard.

Jennifer felt a bit of dust blow into her eyes—or something that felt like dust—and it stung. She rubbed hard at her eyes until the stinging ceased. When it did, Jennifer blinked hard a few times and then looked around.

She suddenly stopped walking, but the others all coaxed frantically for her to keep going. She simply could not. What Jennifer was seeing was so crazy, so unbelievable, so outrageous, that it stopped her in her tracks. She could not take even a small step as long as her eyes were seeing what had come—and what was still coming—to surround her and the others.

"I … they … but …" Jennifer stumbled and stammered over her words because it was clear the others' eyes had not been opened. There were no words that would come to her tongue to explain what she was seeing. She wanted to, but her tongue got twisted up as she tried. The more Jennifer tried to explain it, the more knotted her tongue became. Soon, she gave up entirely.

This only made the other Travelers panic all the more. They worried that the fear had finally gotten too overwhelming and the poor girl had lost her mind.

"Jennifer, get moving!" Judah hollered and grabbed her hand as he went past her.

"Why are you stopping?" Bella demanded to know, now choking on a full portion of dread.

Jennifer heard all of their words and felt herself being pulled along by Judah and Matt. But in her mind, she was in a place altogether different. Time was standing still for her; there was not a trace of panic or a shred of fear for she knew that indeed, Simeon had spread out his wings and covered her beneath them.

"Wait," she said.

Nobody heard her; they were much too busy panicking and trying to pull her along.

"Stop," she said a tad louder. Still, they ignored her. Finally, she pulled her hands away from the boys (although she did consider *not* doing this so that she had an excuse to hold Matt's hand) and shrieked as loud as she could.

"STOOOOPPPP!"

They stopped, but only to look at her. She'd lost her mind. The armies were bearing down on them now; they knew the Travelers had seen them.

"I suppose if our journey must come to an end, then this is how it shall be," Bella cried.

"Bella!" Jennifer rebuked her auntie. "Do you not trust the Shailmas at all?" Of course, it was much easier for Jennifer to trust them since she could see them. None of the others could, but that made no difference to Jennifer right now as she scolded her auntie.

"What?" Bella screeched. "What does that have to do with …" but before Bella could get all her words out, Shura touched her eyes and they, too, were immediately opened and she saw what Jennifer had seen.

Bella fell to her knees and started weeping. She had not trusted the Shailmas after all, and now that she had seen them, she felt terribly shameful and filled with regret. It was her who had taught Jennifer about the Shailmas, and now it was Jennifer who was teaching her.

None of the other Travelers' eyes had been opened to what was on the other side of the air, but the Army of Shrailzhar saw. There was no doubt about it for in an instant, they tried to stop; the entire army dug in their heels and tried to turn back. It took a few minutes to do so —since they were great in number—and many of them got trampled in the process. The army did eventually manage to get themselves stopped, but by the time they did, they were close to the Travelers.

Those Travelers who had not seen what Jennifer and Bella saw were so confused they didn't even know what questions to ask. They stumbled on their words and the girls could see the others' eyes were all filled with terror even though the army had stopped and were now retreating.

"Jennifer?" Judah asked.

"Bella?" Pierce added.

"You can't see it?" Bella whispered. She was still on her knees sobbing from the great disappointment she had in herself.

"See what?" Sam asked.

"Why did the army stop? Why are they going the other way?" Pierce wanted to know.

It was clear they were all becoming frustrated, and they were already very angry, so the girls tried their best to explain what was truly unexplainable. Nonetheless, they tried their best.

"You mean there are hundreds of Shailmas around us?" Sam finally blurted out. He sounded doubtful of what Jennifer had said, but then again, since there was no other explanation for what was happening with Shrailzhar's Army, he didn't have much of a choice.

"No," Jennifer said. "That's not what I mean—exactly." She grinned, and they thought for certain this time, she'd lost her mind.

"More like thousands of Shailmas," Bella explained. "Far too many for us to count." She jumped up from her knees, wiped her tears, and began to jump for joy as more and more and more of the Shamar Shailmas surrounded the tiny group. Jennifer giggled.

"Far too many for us to even see!" she added.

The girls went on and on, back and forth with their giggles and explanations until finally, Pierce had enough of their foolish antics.

"You're telling me," he huffed, "there are thousands—or more —of the Shailmas that have come and surrounded us?" Now his voice rose about two octaves when he asked the next question.

"And you can SEE them?"

"Yup," Jennifer announced. "That's exactly what we are telling you. We're surrounded by an endless circle of Shailmas, and the army can see them too, apparently. They are the Warring Shamar Shailmas," she added, just in case he cared to know such details which in this outlandish moment, he did not.

They all stood there; dumbfounded with so much to say yet no words to say any of it.

"I saw these, not this many of course, but a dozen I think it was, when I was in the adder's pit!" Jennifer got excited all over again when she remembered how Simeon had called for those Shamar Shailmas to come and surround her when King Shrailzhar was after her.

"If I didn't see it with my own eyes," Bella announced, for she could see how doubtful the rest were, "I'd not believe it either. But we're telling you the truth." The others were believing them because there was no other explanation for the army to have stopped so quickly and retreat so far back.

With Bella's last statement, the eyes of her heart closed and the Warring Shamar Shailmas were once more hidden from her sight.

"Aw," she sighed. It didn't take her long to go from completely believing, to being a little unsure. While she could see the Shamar Shailmas, it was easy for her to believe. When she could no longer see them surrounding her, she struggled to believe they were still there.

Is it me that no longer sees them? she wondered, or *they, that are no longer here.* She couldn't determine which it was so she decided to watch Jennifer and see if she could figure it out from there. Jennifer could still see them and it filled her with confidence just like it had in the adder's pit. Suddenly, a lesson from the adder's pit came to her. Something she'd learned there was now necessary to remember here …

"When we cannot see the Shailmas anymore, then we need to watch the army," she explained. "If they are not chasing us, if they back off, then it's clear the Shailmas are still surrounding us."

While it made much sense to some, a bit of sense to a few, and absolutely no sense to the rest, it was still difficult to believe for everyone … everyone that is, except for Jennifer. What was about to make matters worse was that Pierce refused to believe it at all.

"If my eyes can't see it I will not believe it," he blurted, which, of course, was the worst thing any of them could have said.

All is Well

7

"No ..." Jennifer commanded. "Do NOT say such a thing!" For a reason nobody could understand, Pierce's loud declaration of his unbelief in the Shailmas had stirred something up in Jennifer. If the Army of Shrailzhar had retreated and her fears had calmed, Pierce's unbelief immediately brought those fears right back up. The Travelers looked at Jennifer again with confused expressions. They were beginning to get annoyed with the girl.

"Why not?" Pierce asked. He, nor anybody else, figured that what he said should be a big deal, but Jennifer knew that it was. She became more and more agitated as he continued to talk about his unbelief. She did not particularly understand why this was so, but couldn't deny it was causing great anxiety in her soul and blotted out whatever peace she had managed to hold onto from the Chamber of Rest.

Kaija Mae spoke up softly because there was suddenly great tension between the Travelers and what they needed now was to be united, not torn apart. She didn't want to add to that tension, but nobody seemed to think they should keep heading deeper into the Dark Land. At least nobody was moving …

Have they forgotten we need that last tablet? she wondered.

Kaija Mae's Shailma strongly urged her to get the group moving and so, with the confidence she received from him, she finally spoke up.

"Can you figure this out while we get moving?" she suggested. Kaija Mae was trying to sound as calm as she could make herself sound, but in fact, she too was becoming quite agitated. The Travelers were wasting so much time—the one thing they had very little of. Surely this was not so immediately important that it had to be discussed and figured out this very second.

But it WAS that important.

The Shailmas could not stay where unbelief blocked them out; it was in the realm of belief where they dwelt. Yes; such a thing was of immediate importance indeed. If Pierce continued to doubt his Shailma was present, protecting and leading him, well, then his Shailma could not stay as close as was necessary, and Pierce would be exposed to the army.

Jennifer searched Simeon's thoughts for help. She knew they could not just stand around, even though they were in the midst of the Shamar Shailmas; they had to find the tablet. But she also knew they couldn't keep going as long as Pierce refused to believe, unless they left him behind. Jennifer was not about to do such a thing.

The last clay tablet, Simeon, she cried. *Please show me where to go ... tell me how to convince Pierce ... help me, Simeon ... PLEASE!* Jennifer cried out loud and strong, in that unseen place where the Shailmas lived. She begged and pleaded for him to help her ... to help them.

What she heard in response was not what she'd expected. Jennifer expected Simeon to give her a wonderful lecture about the power of believing which she could pass on to Pierce, making her sound absolutely brilliant. She did not get one. She expected orderly and specific directions, how many steps one way before turning another way, that would lead them straight to the corner and finally to the last tablet. She received no such directions.

What Jennifer did receive, was far greater than anything she'd expected or hoped for. It was a lesson all in itself; the very lesson she wanted Pierce to understand, she was just about to learn herself.

Little One, Simeon began. *You see me with your heart, and for now—for these few moments—you see me with your eyes. Still, you do not believe.*

What? she thought. *That can't be right! I do believe you, Simeon.*

No, Little One, you do not. If you did, you would know I will help you at the perfect time, not necessarily when you demand it. The destination is not always where I am. That is not where the greatest lessons are learned, or the fiercest strength is built. No, Little One. It is in the journey—in the difficulties—where you find out all you must know to make you ready to stand in the destination.

Everything is as it must be, Jenny. Everything is as it must be for the journey to take you to the destination. But only when you keep your eyes on me and trust me completely, can you get there. It is when you turn around or look around you that you feel fear. It is then that you doubt me.

I always lead you, Little One, but often you don't follow.

Jennifer was confused, and annoyed, and relieved. Simeon often talked in riddles it seemed, and Jennifer never prided herself on being too great at solving riddles. However, the one thing she did understand from her Shailma was to trust him. That, she could do—or try to do—and believe Simeon would come through and do the rest.

"I trust you, Simeon," she whispered and at that moment, she did.

Jennifer took a big breath and realized how terrible the air tasted. It wreaked of sulfur, and she wondered why she was just noticing this now, and if anyone else had noticed before now. She spat on the ground to get the taste out of her mouth, and her eyes sprang open when she saw her ball of sulfur-tasting spit sizzle as it hit the dirt, like water sprinkled into a pan of hot oil.

"Um," she whispered with baited shallowness. "Um guys," she said again just a bit louder. Jennifer hoped someone else had seen it and from the looks on their faces, she knew they had. An overwhelming panic draped itself, unwelcome and unwanted, over each Traveler. While Jennifer tried hard to remain calm and trust Simeon, she was having a difficult time doing so. Could this be why he had just given her such a lecture on trusting him? It seemed obvious that Simeon must have known what was about to come and wanted to build more trust in her … and fast.

Simeon, she wailed, *get us out of here. Where is the tablet?*

Jennifer, don't let the circumstances you see around you break your trust in me. She expected her Shailma to sound impatient by now, but as always, his words had no sound of impatience or frustration; only kindness and compassion.

Look around you, Little One, and see what you see. She did, and he opened her eyes once more—just for a momentary flash—and all she saw excited her greatly.

The Shamar Shailmas had doubled in number, and while many were still on the ground surrounding them, others had unfolded their mighty wings and were hovering above them. Indeed, they were surrounded on every side.

Some Shamar Shailmas had riders—each rider was covered in the shiniest silver armor imaginable, waving enormous double-edged swords. The swords were gleaming, even though there was no sun to catch their edges and cause the blinding flashes which shot out like lightning. As Jennifer looked closer at those double-edged swords trying to figure out where the light was coming from, she realized—and it caused her to gasp—that the light WAS the swords.

Every rider also had a shield, so large yet they made it look lighter than air. They were translucent … yet solid … completely unexplainable and Jennifer knew a greater war was brewing in the atmosphere than she'd even considered. Her mind told her to panic; she and the others were the cause of the war, and even worse, they were stuck right in the middle of it. But her heart told her to remain calm, for *all is well*, she heard. *All is well.*

Her eyes moved from above to beneath, and what she saw there persuaded her to panic, yet she refused to, even still. Just below the surface of the ground, churning beneath the dirt, was a simmering sea of reds and oranges and even yellows and a bit of blues and just a hint of greens.

FIRE. She could see it clearly, swirling, and Jennifer knew that was the source of the magnificent heat that made her spit sizzle. Her feet didn't feel it, and she knew it wasn't the big ugly boots of the Travelers protecting her feet because she had lost hers. In fact, her feet had only the tiniest protection from her canvas sneakers, yet they felt no heat whatsoever.

As Jennifer looked around, searching for any reasonable explanation, she suddenly found one. Beneath their feet, shielding them from the heat, were plates. Not the kind one eats from, but more like small panels that were insulated from the extreme heat. They were slightly larger than the size of each one's foot. Jennifer nervously took a step and watched as the plate moved from where her foot was to where it was going. As she set her foot down, the plate slid perfectly underneath, shielding it from the heat. Not even her baby toe touched the ground.

"Unbelievable," she muttered and shook her head. Simeon again veiled her eyes, and everything she'd just seen so plainly was gone from view. She knew it was gone only from her sight, though, and that all that was around them remained, whether or not she could see it. Jennifer could trust Simeon; he would keep them safe.

"What is unbelievable?" Kaija Mae asked. Panic was turning into hysteria among the group. Panic would be a reasonable thing to feel for anyone caught between a deadly army and a scorching heat. Surely they must have been wondering which would be the one to bring them to their end. But it was obvious that Jennifer saw things the rest of them were blinded to, and they watched her face. There was not a trace of panic in Jennifer's gaze. They were going to have to rely on her, which was just one more reason to panic.

"I can't explain it now; we have to move ... quickly!" she shouted.

Jennifer lifted one foot and slowly set it down in front of her. She waited a minute, just to make sure the plates were still shielding her feet now that she could no longer see them. She felt nothing uncomfortable so moved the other foot. Faster and faster she began to move her feet until she was running. As fast as she could go is exactly as fast as she went.

The others took no time to consider why her spit sizzled; they were now right behind her, trying not to outrun her. Even though they could all run much faster than Jennifer, none of them knew which direction to go, so they made sure to stay behind her, even if it was only a step or two. They only assumed, of course, that she knew which way to go but since nobody else wanted to take the lead, they let her and hoped their assumption was right.

Jennifer ran out of breath quickly but kept running for as long as she could. Finally, she slowed down and bent over to catch her breath. The others did the same.

The Travelers had run so far that the flat ground where Malleana Forest used to be—which now had only the hollow coverings dotting the land here and there—were far behind them, but the Army of Shrailzhar was not. They had stayed close to the Travelers, even though they couldn't get at them because of the Shamar Shailmas.

Jennifer, Bella, Pierce, and the others had run straight into a large batch of trees—another forest of some type but not Malleana Forest for it was nothing the same. The trees here were different. They were smoldering from the bottom up, and most had their tops already burned off. They looked like a book of burned-up matches, only tree-sized.

A fire had ripped through this woodland recently, and the heat was still smoldering in the air. It was too warm for the Travelers to keep wearing their heavy cloaks and so, after consulting with the Shailmas and one another, they took the cloaks off and left them on the ground. The Army of Shrailzhar had seen them anyway; the cloaks were not exactly hiding them anymore.

Bella handed the food containers around for each one to carry since there were too many for her to carry by herself.

Matt carried the basket of tablets which would soon become heavy and burdensome without the cloak to bear their weight.

"We'll take turns," Pierce suggested.

"Here," Sam said and held his arms out toward the basket containing the tablets. "I'll carry it." Matt nodded but did not hand them over.

The Travelers kept on going, albeit much slower now. They were tired from running, nervous without their cloaks, and the smoldering trees were close together, making it difficult to move quickly. Furthermore, the smoke from the trees made their breathing raspy and laborious. Some yanked their sleeves down, and others pulled their shirts over their mouths to try and keep as much of the sulfur and smoke from their noses as was possible.

Matt turned around to look back at the cloaks and shouted when he saw them. The ground had set them on fire and the army had picked them up, put them on poles, and were carrying those cloaks, which had once been the Travelers' safe covering, like flags—burning flags. Kaija Mae turned around as well and saw the sight. She started shaking a little, but Jennifer grabbed her arm.

"Don't look back," she scolded. "NEVER LOOK BACK," Jennifer shouted to the others.

But Kaija Mae couldn't help it; what she'd seen of the army had hooked into her soul and refused to let go. It was calling to her now; she could hear it.

Jennifer knew something was wrong and grabbed Kaija Mae by the face. She looked straight into the girl's eyes and said nothing for a long moment.

Finally, she said, "SING, KAIJA MAE. YOU HAVE TO SING."

So Kaija Mae sang.

Sulphur Burning

8

Kaija Mae sang at the top of her lungs. Usually, she was quiet; it was just her nature to be quiet. But not this time. This time she shouted and sang and sang and shouted. Of course, nobody could sing along since nobody had any idea what she was singing. Even though what came from her was unimaginably beautiful, none of her songs ever had understandable words.

For that matter, even Kaija Mae didn't know the words since she had never learned the languages in which her songs were sung. When she sang, she would just open her mouth and the words would come out. She put the tunes together but not the words. They flowed really, as though she'd known the songs forever.

Kaija Mae didn't understand and thought of it as a gift of some sort. It had been that way ever since she was dragged from her home so long ago to this horrible land of Trilleah. She didn't mind such a gift at all and was quite thankful; she'd learned her songs brought peace to troubled souls and sometimes, healing to broken bodies. It was undoubtedly an unbelievable, unexplainable gift, and she was glad to have it.

The land had changed drastically since that day she'd arrived so many years before. Kaija Mae had spent over sixty years believing she would never get out of this Dark Land. She'd met up with the king more than once, and had escaped him each time. The old woman—who was in the body of a young lady—had so many stories to tell. She had seen so much in this Dark Land of Trilleah but had no time to share any of it with anyone else.

Maybe one day, she thought.

Kaija Mae had never told any of the Travelers of the biggest secret she knew—not even Judah. She had waited for the right time to tell them, but so far that time had not come. She doubted she would ever find an appropriate time to tell them that they were not the first ones to be brought to Trilleah or that all those other hollows they'd seen earlier this morning were for other Travelers, just like themselves; Travelers who no longer needed those hollows.

She had never told them because she was afraid of scaring them off. Kaija Mae was terrified to let them know that so many others had come before them and had lost their battle with the king. She feared if they knew, they would not return. She couldn't bring herself to tell them that all those other Curse Breakers never had a chance to break the curse because the army had gotten ahold of them and they were now part of Malleana Forest. They had joined the Waiting Ones.

Maybe one day she'd tell them, but this was not that day.

As they wandered along, being led by Jennifer—who was being led by Simeon—Kaija Mae continued to sing. It was terribly eerie and painfully quiet, weaving in and out of these smoldering, broken bits and pieces of trees. There was something about them that made everyone a whole lot uneasy. It felt like the trees were watching them, but that seemed silly. The smell of sulfur was so strong it burned their throats, making them cough uncontrollably.

Still, there was something uneasy that the Travelers couldn't shake. It was like the smoldering trees, broken and burned up, were playing a game of some sort with them—a game they'd rather not play. As the Travelers would wander through the woodlands and leave a large group of the smoldering and burning trees behind, it would not be but a little while and those they'd passed seemed to be in front of them again.

Over and over and over again, it seemed like this was what was happening.

"That one looks familiar," Judah said, pointing at one tree in particular.

"So does that one," Bella said pointing to another.

"I'm sure we already passed this way," Matt mentioned more than once.

"We are nearly out of these smothering woods," Jennifer shouted back. As she looked ahead, she could see a small clearing. But by the time she would get to the clearing, it would be crowded out with trees again. It made no sense and she stopped to turn and see if she was leading the others round and round in one giant circle.

She definitely was not, but then as they would look back it seemed there were very few of the broken, smoldering trees behind them even though they knew they'd journeyed through many. It made their heads spin, confusing them thoroughly.

"This makes no sense," Pierce complained. The others agreed.

"I feel like I keep seeing the same trees over and over again," Judah added. Bella nodded, and Sam shrugged his shoulders. "I know I'm lost!" he said.

"I feel lost too," Jennifer moped, "but I know this is the right way."

"The right way to where?" Judah huffed. "Where are we going, because it feels like we are just wandering around hoping we might get somewhere when, in fact, we are getting closer and closer to nowhere at all!

"This is where Simeon is leading me, Judah," his sister complained. "If you want to go first, I'm perfectly fine with that."

Jennifer stopped and stepped aside, giving Judah space to go past her. He didn't.

Judah felt bad, but only slightly. He was tired and hungry; everyone was. But what Jennifer didn't know—and she probably never would—was that last night while some of them slept on the cave floor, Judah didn't. He didn't close his eyes for even a minute. Instead, he sat against a wall right inside of the entrance of the cave and watched.

He had no idea what he was watching for, but he knew after seeing his sister get swallowed up by the earth on the last journey, he was not about to let anything into the cave that might drag her away; not this time. Judah had every intention of doing whatever was necessary to keep that cave safe for his sister while she got some rest.

Judah had waited until they were all asleep, and then he snuck back out into the howling winds and hurling lightning. Yes, Jennifer's brave brother crawled around on his hands and knees for a long time until he'd found a jagged rock. Then, he spent a long while rubbing it on a rough boulder making it razor sharp. Nothing was going to take his sister from him again; he'd make sure of that.

Thankfully, nothing had ventured into the cave while the others slept, and Judah was glad. Now, though, he was beginning to feel the effects of missing out on the sleep the others had attained in the night. His stomach growled and he thought he could not take one more step until he put either rest in his bones or some food in his belly. There was no resting to be done, so he opted for the food.

"Bella," he moaned, "I have GOT to eat something!"

"I was thinking the same thing," Pierce said. "My stomach is beginning to eat itself." Well, that was a bit of an exaggeration, but Pierce wanted to make his point.

"Where would you suppose we stop to eat?" Bella asked. As she was looking around for a spot, she thought she saw a large pair of eyes just beyond the last row of smoldering trees. She watched for a minute—just long enough to see them blink—then quickly looked away. *Please, please don't see us,* she quietly begged. *Shura,* she cried, *hide us from whatever is staring at us.*

"Um," she stuttered, "I think we should go over here," and she pointed in the opposite direction of the eyes that she was pretending not to have seen. Bella was sure she had seen something blink but tried to convince herself it was just her imagination getting the best of her. She ignored it, not mentioning it to anyone except Shura, and instead moved to a faraway spot that had a tiny opening.

"Set the containers here," Bella said as she set the one she'd been carrying down with a bit of a thud. Her hands were shaking terribly, but nobody noticed. Jennifer had been looking around as well, trying to figure out which was the way out of these eerie trees. Out of the corner of her eye, she saw Bella stoop over to set the container down. Before she could holler at her not to, the container touched the ground and within seconds, the bottom of it melted out, and the food went up in a quick burst of flames.

"Oh no," Jennifer sighed. She knew now that she should have told the others about what Simeon had shown her under the ground— and about the insulating pads that she'd seen under their feet.

"WHAT HAPPENED?" Pierce shouted.

"THE FOOD!" Judah cried.

They tried to pick up what they could from the melted container, but there was nothing left worth salvaging. The others were glad they had not yet set their containers down and held them tightly against their chests.

"What happened?" Bella demanded. She sounded angry and Jennifer was nervous now to tell them what she'd seen earlier. She hesitated. She knew they'd be angry with her for not telling them before some of the food was destroyed—even though she was only trying to keep them from worrying. But now, her reasons for not telling them didn't matter. Their food was half gone, and no one was happy about it. They would surely blame her and Jennifer grew anxious.

"You see," she stared down at the ground; she couldn't bear to look anyone in the eye. "Simeon showed me that right below this layer of ground is a sea—an enormous sea—covering nearly the entire belly of the land. But there is this thin layer of ground laid over it." Jennifer paused, contemplating how best to say what she knew she must.

"It's a sea of fire," she finally whispered.

"A sea of WHAT?" Pierce shrieked. "There is no way I heard you right," he demanded. He was angry and really, she couldn't blame him or any of the others for being upset with her. She had thought keeping such information to herself was a wise choice; now she realized it was incredibly foolish.

Jennifer took as much time as it took them to eat the rest of their food—which wasn't much, so it didn't take long—to tell them what she'd seen earlier. She told them about the Shamar Shailmas that were still hovering above them now, and about their armor, and the double-edged swords of light which they held.

Then, she told them in as much detail as she possibly could recall, about the Sea of Acheron she'd seen below them and the insulated plates that were beneath their feet. "And so that's why the container melted and the food was ruined," she said. "I'm so sorry," she sulked and looked back to the ground, hanging her head as if it was all her fault when, in fact, none of it was.

Most of them were speechless. After all, what does one say to such a thing? Pierce found something to say, and although he said it kindly and put his arm around Jennifer when he said it, she wasn't sure if he was joking to lighten the mood or if he was serious but used a kind tone so that she was less offended.

"Well, Jenny, there's only one explanation for such things. Obviously, you're crazy!" he said.

There was no squeezing her shoulder or mischievous grin or playful wink to indicate he was just playing, so she had to think he meant it and her feelings were offended. After all, she couldn't help what Simeon chose to show her. She couldn't help that the other Shailmas didn't show their riders such things. Jennifer couldn't help that there was a lake of fire beneath the ground they stood on, or that there were insulated plates beneath their feet. She couldn't help any of it. She certainly didn't ask to know such things or see such things or be the leader of all this horror.

But then, that silly Pierce did a foolish thing. He bent down and mockingly said, "so if I do this then, my finger should burn up," and he poked his finger into the ground. Before even one second could pass, Pierce shrieked and jumped back. He held out his finger to see that the end of it, where he had touched it to the ground, was horribly burned and raw where the flesh should be.

"OH NO!" Bella hollered.

"WHAT ARE WE GOING TO DO?" Sam screamed. He, too, began jumping around like a lunatic—like the ground was going to do the same thing to his feet. The poor boy expected himself to melt into a pool of skin and bones any second now.

Did they not hear what I just told them? Jennifer wondered. She didn't have a chance to tell them again, however, because as she opened her mouth to repeat herself, she instead heard Simeon break into her thoughts.

It doesn't feel very good, does it? he asked.

What doesn't feel very good? She was confused.

When you tell them something so important and they act as if you never told them ... or like they don't believe you ... or that they know better than you.

Oh, she sulked. Jennifer understood what he was saying, and agreed that it was hurtful. She realized that must be how Simeon felt when she acted like she didn't believe him, and she vowed to change it.

Little One, Simeon said boldly. *You are a Princess Warrior. There is nothing you cannot do if you trust me.* Jennifer didn't respond because she didn't know what a Princess Warrior was, and she was certain that she didn't want to know. Jennifer wasn't sure what "nothing you cannot do" might include and right now, she was happier not knowing such things. Whatever a Princess Warrior was, she was sure that she was not it.

Instead of trying to figure any of it out, Jennifer tried again to tell the others about the plates under their feet and reassure them that as long as they stayed on their feet, they were safe. Jennifer reminded them that if they would believe what she was telling them—because she'd seen it with her own eyes, after all—that they would be safe from whatever might rage beneath them, whether it was seen things or unseen things.

She wanted to believe it herself just as much as she wanted those listening to believe it. The problem was, she didn't … neither did the others.

Hush Now

9

Kaija Mae's songs brought a wee amount of comfort to the group and although they were all still deeply disturbed, and Pierce was in horrible pain, a little comfort was better than no comfort at all.

Judah moved closer to his sister. Even though he was still upset with her because he was hungry, he couldn't blame her for not sharing with the others what she'd seen. He knew she always worried about such things, thinking the others would find her to be a lunatic, and he was sure—without her saying so—that this was the reason she'd kept silent on the matter of the lake of fire.

"Jelly Bean," he whispered. "I'm sorry for the weight of such a heavy responsibility that you must be carrying. If I could take it from you and lead us to the tablet, I would."

Jennifer became teary-eyed at her brother's words. She was feeling desperately alone until he spoke such confidence to her. She was sure nobody could understand the heaviness of all that laid on her shoulders, but it seemed that, just maybe, Judah did. And if he didn't fully understand it, he was trying, and that made her feel a little less alone.

That was more than anyone else was doing and being truthful, Jennifer was disappointed in her auntie. It was Bella who had brought her here without asking her or explaining anything about any of this. Bella hadn't even let her ask any questions for the longest time. But now, when the journey was getting so hard, harder than anyone ever considered it would become, Jennifer felt like Bella was turning on her, or maybe even abandoning her.

"Thank you, Judah," she whispered and grabbed his hand. "Stay with me, will you?" she sulked.

"Of course," he replied and squeezed her hand.

"Do you know which way to go?" he asked. "Oh, and don't mind Pierce or any of the others. They are just scared and blaming you. They don't know what they're doing at all!"

"No; I don't know which way to go. It seems like every direction I feel like Simeon leads me is the wrong way. And Judah," she stopped and looked him in the eye. "I don't care if they're scared because I'm scared too. I'm the one who got pulled into the adder's pit, and I'm the one who's seen the shells of all those Waiting Ones. I'm the one who has looked into the hollow eyes of that dreadful, stupid king."

He squeezed her hand again, and she turned back and continued walking.

Bella looked over to the right, where she had seen the eyes blinking earlier. She hoped not to see them again. She hoped those eyes were gone or that it was only her imagination going hysterical, but it took no more than a second to find the eyes were still there—still staring. They didn't seem to be moving with the Travelers, rather staring at them from that one spot—watching them. Her belly turned over and her skin felt sticky. *Do I tell the others?* she pleaded with Shura.

Will it help? Shura answered immediately. *Bella, not yet. But keep watch of them ... they are certainly keeping watch of you.*

That didn't help calm her at all, but Bella was going to do what Shura had told her. She was going to keep a close watch on the eyes that were keeping a close watch on her.

So on it went.

Bella was watching the pair of eyes that was watching the Travelers. Judah was trying to keep Jennifer from completely panicking and giving up. Sam was looking at his feet, trying hard to see the insulated plates keeping his shoes from burning up. Matt was extraordinarily careful trying to keep the basket of clay tablets safe.

Pierce was wincing and holding his finger up trying not to bump it, and Kaija Mae was singing her songs.

There were others who'd been traveling with Kaija Mae for much longer than any of the other Travelers had even been in the land, and they were trying to avoid talking or whining or panicking. They too had seen many other Travelers come and go, and they were at the peak of concern now that these ones—these Travelers who were so close to the end of this journey—would not make it either. This was their last hope of ever getting out of Trilleah, that much was clear.

Everyone was doing something, so the quiet was much appreciated by Jennifer. She was talking and listening continually with her Shailma, trying to figure out what a Princess Warrior was and begging him to show her the way out of this hot, smelly, smoky woodland. Her eyes were burning from the sulfur and her throat was dreadfully sore.

Simeon, our time is running out, and I can't hear you. Why aren't you showing me the way? Jennifer whined. *Now, in the hardest bit of this utterly dreadful journey, are you going to leave me? SIMEON? SIMEON!!!*

You're not listening, is what she finally heard. Jennifer wanted to argue but knew there was no time for that. She never won arguments with Simeon anyway.

Instead, she whispered, "I'm sorry, I really am. I'm trying so hard to listen, but there's so much noise in my head that I can't hear you."

Jenny, Simeon replied so softly, *you can't listen harder, you can only quiet all the other things in your mind so there is a space for my voice. You will never hear me over worries and fears. Put those things away now so you can hear me.*

She did. One by one, Jennifer pictured herself taking all the things crowding out Simeon's voice and setting them high on a shelf in the very back corner of her mind.

Stay there, she commanded fear.

Do not come down, she told worries.

Don't bother me again, she scolded the heaviness of all she'd seen earlier. In her imagination she closed the doors, shutting all those things behind them and then, albeit just in her imagination, Jennifer hung a gigantic lock on the doors. *Click* went the lock in her mind.

And now, my dear Simeon, I see you clearly. I am listening carefully, so please tell me which way to go and how to get out of this woodland.

He did. The trees stood still and continued to smolder and smell and snap in pieces. Within a few minutes, Simeon led Jennifer—who led the others—safely out of the burned-up forest. They stepped out of that dreadful woodland and danced and jumped and celebrated. It seemed with all that was now behind the Travelers, that they surely must be nearing the tablet. They celebrated far too early, however, for King Shrailzhar was still watching closely. Bella knew it too; she had seen him even though she didn't realize it was he who had been watching them so closely.

The king was in the midst of his army and he was ferociously … viciously … outrageously … angry.

"YOU ARE SUPPOSED TO BE CAPTURING THOSE WRETCHED CURSE BREAKERS," he was screaming. "WHAT IS WRONG WITH YOU BUNCH OF INCOMPETENT, IDIOTIC, BRAINLESS WEASELS? HOW IS IT THAT ALL OF YOU—AN ENTIRE ARMY—ARE INCAPABLE OF CAPTURING A HANDFUL OF PATHETIC, MEASLY, UNARMED CHILDREN?"

Oh yes, King Shrailzhar was angry. He was yelling so loudly that Trilleah again began to shake. It seemed the king himself had set up that smoldering woodland as a trap to catch the Travelers, but when they exited safely on the other side, it infuriated the king even more.

"But your highness," the leader of the army muttered with no courage whatsoever, "they are surrounded by a great cloud of Shamar Warrior Shailmas. We cannot get close to them."

"SILENCE!" King Shrailzhar raged. He disturbed the land again, causing an enormous chunk of the gray sky to fall to the ground, making a large crater in the thin layer of earth. The Sea of Acheron that was hiding just beneath, bubbled over and lapped up onto the dry land. Immediately, it burned every speck of ground that it touched.

The king lowered his voice. Even though he was still raging, he calmed himself a great deal for he was not ready to give up this battle and have his kingdom of Trilleah destroyed. He still hoped they could capture the curse breakers.

"What was that?" Sam shouted as the land rumbled and the sky fell. Trilleah had calmed back down and things were still—or nearly still—once more. For how long, none of them knew.

"I ... I don't know," Judah stammered. "Jennifer, we've got to move faster," he whispered.

They did move faster, but with chunks of the ground-breaking off here and there, it was hard to know exactly where to step. The land was becoming more and more dangerous to be in, and more than anything, the Travelers wanted to get out. As they stepped carefully, jumping over this steaming crack and that blistering crater, the most beautiful singing erupted and everyone became just a little bewildered at the sound of Kaija Mae's incredible song.

One day, after they were long gone from this land, and the tablet was found, and the curse was broken, they were going to ask Kaija Mae about her songs for they undoubtedly came from somewhere far, far away. But not right now. Definitely, not right now.

All the while, the king raged on. He had lowered his voice so Trilleah would not be as disturbed, but the armies knew he was angry with them.

"Did you not see which hollow they came out of?" he seethed. Black smoke flew from his nostrils as he raged quietly at the General of his army.

"We did, your majesty," the Army General said. He was so afraid the king would smite him dead, that he held his shield over his head as he spoke, just in case Shrailzhar did not like something he said and decided to bring his sword down on the General's head.

"Well then WHY, tell me, did you not kill those wretched little urchins when you had the chance? TELL ME," he hollered, letting his violent anger rage out of control again.

Trilleah shook. More sky fell from above. More craters opened up in the ground below. More terror filled the Travelers' veins.

Another of the army stepped forward and knelt down on one knee, also covering himself with his shield. "We were busy destroying their hollow," he said cautiously. "Like you directed us to do, oh king."

It seemed the king did not appreciate such an answer because he did bring his sword down on the one who dared to answer his question. The head of that one hit the ground hard and rolled away. The headless soldier slumped over, dead.

The king lifted his bloodied sword toward the sky and shouted. Hundreds of enormous strikes of lightning suddenly burst through the broken sky and struck down one-third of the army. Some fell beneath their shields, and the rest were swept away by a great and powerful wind.

"Useless," the king muttered. "Completely useless!"

He looked over to his closest allies who were surrounding him. "I simply cannot ask this useless army to do anything," he stated harshly. "How are we going to trap those dreadful Curse Breakers?" he demanded. "HOW?"

Now, all those who were surrounding the king and sitting on tremendously large black beasts, looked to one another. While they were all terribly frightening beings themselves, there was none so frightening as the king. They knew fully that if they couldn't come up with a good answer to his question, they, too, would lose their heads.

"Oh great and mighty King Shrailzhar," said the only one who dared to answer. "I believe we must summon all the Nakah Warriors of the air to war with the Shamars." He pointed his sword toward the army and continued. "An army ten times the size of this one could not defeat the Shamar Warriors, your highness."

"Yes," agreed one.

"First, destroy the Shamars," shouted another.

"Or they must be distracted," suggested a third. They all spoke with fear and trembling, for the king was so unpredictable that he could smite any one of them—or all of them—in a moment and without cause, if he chose to.

He didn't. Shrailzhar seemed satisfied with their answers and so, the king let them live.

"YES!" King Shrailzhar agreed excitedly. "You are exactly correct," he said.

With such brilliant suggestions, he looked to Bahlmish, his Chief Executive Sergeant, and demanded firmly, "Summon all the Nakah Warriors to come and battle against the Shamars … at once."

Bahlmish took six of the king's top horsemen, and they rode quickly in search of the Nakah Warriors. They would summon them straightaway—or as soon as they could be located—and the greatest war of all time—the War of the Firmament—would begin.

Gibberish

10

Bahlmish instructed two of the horsemen to ride north, two to ride south, and two to ride east. He went west. They were all in search of the same thing—those Nakah Warriors. There was no way the army could get close to the Travelers unless the Nakahs were successful in taking out a large number of the Shamars or distracting them long enough to get to the Travelers.

At precisely the same moment as those seven horsemen turned to go the directions they were instructed, Matt turned around. They had all heard a great clattering in the skies just behind them, and his curiosity got the best of him. Jennifer immediately warned them to keep looking straight ahead and not look behind, but Matt couldn't help himself.

The warning to look ahead had not come from Simeon specifically. However, Jennifer's memory brought up the time when the Shailmas were carrying them through the portal and Simeon had warned her sharply not to look back. She had, of course, and in her disobedience had caught the eye of the two Nakah Warriors who'd been stationed at the front door of their little yellow house on the corner of Mitchell Avenue and Fairview Lane.

Matt didn't listen now any more than she had listened then, but he quickly wished he had. Bella didn't turn to see what was causing such a ruckus but instead watched Matt's face as he turned. From the look that splattered across it, Bella knew she didn't want to turn around. She saw every drop of color leave him instantly. Even his eyes seemed to go from the beautiful blue that she had admired hundreds of times, to a colorless gray. The blue drained out right before her eyes.

Before she turned to see what she already knew she didn't want to see, Bella glanced toward the eyes of the one that had been watching her. They were gone—at least she couldn't see them, so she assumed they had left. Oh, how she wanted to believe that was a good thing, but the ache rising in her belly told her something altogether different.

Matt continued to look behind him because he was unable to turn away and finally, Bella turned—slowly—to see what had stolen the color from her handsome friend's face. No sooner had her eyes spotted what he was looking at, then she'd wished she had not turned to look.

"Oh, why didn't I listen," she whispered.

In the sky—just a few hundred meters behind them—seven of the biggest, blackest beasts she had ever seen or heard of or even considered, were charging in all directions. She'd never seen anything of the sort! Even the most awful movies she'd snuck into as a little girl did not have such hideous creatures as these. She was horrified beyond words.

These beasts, while resembling something of dragon-like creatures, had the most grotesque features far beyond one's ability to imagine. Their heads were half the size of their bodies, and they didn't have the usual toes of a dragon. Rather, on the ends of their legs where simple toes should have been, were claws. They were more like that of a vulture or a bear, but claws nonetheless.

Bella could tell, even from a distance, that the ends of those claws were razor sharp. Something reminded her of the claws that had tried to carry Jennifer off on another journey, and she shuddered at the thought of it. Her cloak had been torn to shreds; these claws would assuredly be able to skin the Travelers alive.

They had no skin covering the bottom halves of their faces. It looked like there may have been skin there at one time but not anymore. Large chunks were hanging down; it was disgusting, yet she couldn't look away.

Where the lips and skin of these dragons should have been, there were just flaps of something she couldn't quite make out, hanging down from above the teeth. It was grotesque; purely dreadful. Oh, and those teeth. Even from this distance, Bella could see they were sharp and jagged—like the edges of a broken bottle. There was no question in her mind that those teeth would easily rip the flesh off a bear if given a chance.

The very worst of all the features—and there were many—came to Bella's sight as the beasts turned to go in different directions. As each one turned, their tails—which were long and full of motion—stared right back at Bella and began snapping at her. The tails of each of these creatures were made up of a dozen black serpents; their orange eyes pierced Bella's own. She scratched at her eyes and began wiping them fiercely. As she had seen those serpents—as they had seen her—sharp, stabbing pains shot through her eyes and clear through to her brain. Oh, the intense anguish of that pain …

"What happened?" Bella shrieked. She could no longer see anything, although she could feel her hands getting damp as the continued scratching hard at her eyes.

Matt's eyes jolted from the dragons to Bella, and from the reaction she could hear going on around her, Bella knew something drastic had happened. She began screaming and clawing at her eyes—terrified and unable to catch her breath—or see anything whatsoever.

By now, the rest of the Travelers had stopped and were twisting themselves around to see what the commotion was about.

They too wished they hadn't, but it was too late now. Besides, there was no other option.

They ran to Bella, who couldn't see them. Jennifer grabbed her auntie's hands and pulled them away from her eyes because she didn't know if the blood that was dripping down her aunties chin was coming from the claw marks she was making on her face or from her eyes themselves.

"Bella," Judah whispered calmly, but very firmly, into his auntie's ear. "Tell me what happened."

"Who's holding my hands down?" she demanded instead. Bella was trying to pull them loose, shrieking and jumping around as though something had been shot through her eyes and had entered into her mind, twisting it up. Perhaps it had been.

Matt looked back toward the horsemen as they faded into the distance—or the air. It was impossible to decide which it was. He caught a glimpse of the tails, though, just as they faded, and saw the bloodied fangs of those serpents lash out, taunting him and laughing as Matt cringed. He turned back to Bella who hadn't calmed any. Jennifer was struggling to hold onto her auntie's hands, and Bella continued screaming and trying to pull them away.

"Bella," Judah whispered loud enough that he knew she could hear him. "Calm down." That was the wrong thing to say. It was like pouring gas on a fire and expecting it to put out the flame. It had the exact opposite reaction, and Bella upped her volume a great amount.

Now Pierce tried to help. He stepped up and took Bella's hands in his own. He winked at Jennifer and she stepped back enough to let him move in.

"Bella," Pierce said firmly. He waited, but she didn't calm even slightly. "This is not working," he said, looking around at the others whose own eyes had grown large; panic was setting in quickly. They'd all lost their breath and were fighting to get it back, but alarm squeezed in tightly, making it hard.

He put his arms around Bella, tucking her arms inside of his own so she could not lift her hands to claw at her face any longer. The blood slowed, but Pierce's baby blue shirt was catching the drops that did continue to fall.

The tall, strangely handsome young man pulled her close and leaned down to whisper in her ear. As he did, he heard the sweetest of Kaija Mae's tunes being released into the air behind him. He was filled with courage as the unknown words drifted into his soul.

"Now, Bella," he whispered.

He waited for her to calm enough to hear him.

"Bella," he said again. "Listen to me." He had no idea what words he could come up with to help the poor girl, and as he continued to wait for her to calm down, he begged his Shailma for help.

Time was ticking loudly. It was almost as if the ears of the Travelers—and the king—could hear it counting down.

Tick … tick … tick … tick.

Everyone knew such terrible dilemmas could cause long distractions and time could run out. The land would be no more, and the souls would be lost … eternally gone … the Travelers included.

It was because of this piece of knowledge that every single Traveler, even those who did not seek their Shailmas often, desperately sought them now. All the while, King Shrailzhar kept his eyes planted on the Travelers, not realizing what they were doing. Kaija Mae sang softly, and Pierce kept Bella tightly in his embrace. The longer he held her, quietly whispering her name, the calmer her spirit grew and the quieter she became.

Finally, Kaija Mae stopped singing and spoke softly but with such confidence that everyone knew the wisdom came from Shekinah, and wasn't her own. The problem was that the words she uttered were of the same nature with which she sang, so nobody could understand any of it.

They looked around as she spoke because they knew without any shred of doubt that the words were indeed the right ones. They had brought peace, much like that from the Chamber of Rest. Now to figure out what they meant.

"Does anybody have any idea what that means?"

One shook their head; another shrugged their shoulders. Still, someone else said, "uh uh," and one more ran their fingers through their hair in frustration. The rest just stared and looked at the sky or the ground.

It was Bella who finally answered because Shura had interpreted the words for her.

"It means," she declared boldly, without sight and suddenly unafraid, "Follow me. Have no fear; I will be all that you need. I will make straight for you a way in the desert. When the sea rises too high, I will lift you out and carry you on the wings of eagles. Do not be afraid; I am your shield and your buckler. I have gone before you, and I am your rear guard. No weapon raised against you will defeat you, for I am on your side. Though the land shakes and the heavens quiver, I am your victory. Follow me."

As soon as she spoke out the words Shura had put into her heart, her eyes stopped burning, and her sight was returned. What she heard in her heart filled her bones with courage. Bella heard her Shailma whisper in her ear, "Because you have spoken those things I gave you to speak, your sight is returned, and you will lead those who are blind."

That made no sense to her, but really, nothing made sense. Much of what she'd told the Travelers—who were still looking at her like she was either a complete lunatic or an angel from God—sounded like foolish gibberish.

Bella wished Pierce hadn't let go of her so quickly because she was rather enjoying being close to him. Although Matt was the one who had her heart, Pierce was a close second. There was something about him, though, the tiniest of things really, that unsettled her. It might have been the odd haircut or the tattoos; she wasn't sure. Bella just knew there was something about him that didn't sit right in her belly.

Bella looked at her bloodied hands. She saw that under her fingernails she had pieces of her own flesh and realized she must have looked awful. Her eyes still stung, but not nearly as much as a few minutes ago. And, she could see. There was not much more she could ask for right now.

Jennifer was anxious to keep moving. Once again the sun had gotten to the top of the land and was quickly falling back down, heading to the horizon. Nobody knew for certain if it mattered anymore but nevertheless, it was wise for them to move quickly.

"Let's go," Bella said as she turned and began to move speedily.

Giving Notice

11

King Shrailzhar had been watching all these goings-on and what Bella didn't know—there was no way she possibly could—was that the king had directed those horsemen to put a "blinding" curse on her. Of course, she thought it was from the serpents that were twisted into the tails of the dragon beasts, and that is what she'd eventually tell the others.

However, it was not the serpents since they had no power to call for such a curse. The king knew that Bella had seen him earlier, watching the Travelers, and so he empowered his horsemen to close the eyes of that one who'd dared to look at him.

Now, it must be said that the king had the power to end the journey of every Traveler, just as he had with the Travelers who had trespassed on his Dark Land in the past. However, the Shamar Shailmas had now joined forces and had been covering these Travelers far too consistently for the king to get near enough to them. That's exactly why Shrailzhar had instructed his armies to do it. The king was not about to do battle with the Shamars, which was why he had put in order the Army of Trilleah well over fifty years ago. He had brought them together and had Bahlmish train them up in war, for such a time as this.

Clearly, his greatest Chief Executive Sergeant had not trained them well enough. The one time—this very moment for which they were trained—when King Shrailzhar had called upon them, that dreadful army failed him miserably.

Because of their horrible failure, the king debated whether to strike them all down, to drag his devilish arm across the land and swipe them all into the Sea of Acheron—or let the remaining two-thirds of his army carry on. Shrailzhar decided he may need them yet before he set up his final kingdom for eternity, so he let them keep their breath—and their heads—for now.

King Shrailzhar was getting impatient. What was taking Bahlmish so long to call together the Nakah Warriors? He let his impatience get the best of him and threw his head back, releasing the most outrageous howl Trilleah had ever heard.

The Dark Land shook … hard. The Travelers were nearly thrown to the ground, which would have been treacherous with the Sea of Acheron bubbling beneath the surface. If one measly second of contact with the ground did such damage to Pierce's finger, there was no telling what damage would be done if the Travelers were shaken off their feet and thrown to the ground.

Judah wobbled. Sam toppled but caught himself before he completely lost his balance. Bella teetered and fell against Pierce. Everyone held their breath until they regained their balance, but the ground kept right on shaking. They had heard the king's wailings as well, and the Travelers knew they were in trouble.

Jennifer looked up and saw nothing other than bits of the sky that continued to crumble. She looked behind and in front, and saw nothing more than the air that was sending up billows of sulfuric smoke. When the winds would rise, pieces of trees and ash from the burned woodlands would swirl, but for now, the winds were still.

Even though she didn't see the Shamar Shailmas surrounding them, Jennifer knew they must be there. If they were not—if for some reason they had left the Travelers unprotected—she was sure the Army of Shrailzhar would overtake them in seconds. She may not have seen the Shailmas, but the army did, and she heard Simeon's whisper.

Jennifer, this way, he said to her. She looked "this way," and it did not look like any way they may want to venture. "This way," was bubbling. "This way, " had sulfur rising; not little puffs like they'd seen earlier, but the entire ground was covered. They'd not be able to see where they were stepping if they went the way Simeon was suggesting.

"This way, " looked like a mist was rising and covering at least three feet above the ground, only that mist was not a mist. It was smoke and sulfur from the Sea of Acheron that was beginning to rise.

Simeon! she hesitated. *You cannot be serious ... we can't go that way. It's too dangerous!*

Jennifer, I would not lead you anywhere that I will not give you what you need to go, he replied. *There's nowhere you can go where I will not be with you.* They discussed and debated back and forth but the clock was still ticking and the sands of time were running out.

Okay, Simeon, Jennifer sighed with a heavy heart. *I'll go where you tell me to go, but I doubt the others will follow.*

They'll follow you because they trust you, Simeon answered her.

Sigh. *We'll see ...* Jennifer breathed hard and took a step in the direction Simeon had pointed her. Nobody followed. She took another step and still nobody was behind her. Another step and another step and another and one more. She dared not look behind, both for fear that none were with her—and for fear that they were. It was not her decision to lead the others; it was put upon her, and she was scared—oh, so scared. If she heard wrong, if she led them in the wrong direction ... she dared not even consider such a dreadful thought.

"Jennifer," she heard from behind her. "We're with you." It was Judah. Her heart beat loudly and she could hear it in her ears. One misstep—only one—and they would either fall to what was below … or that which was below would rise and overtake them.

"Why me?" she begged of Simeon as he led her to the next step to place her feet where it was safe; firm and steady.

"Because you listen," he said. He didn't speak silently in her mind where he usually spoke, but loudly into her ears. "In the loudness and commotion of all that is around you, Little One, you have learned to shut it out and hear my voice. The others haven't learned to do that."

His words moved now, back into her mind where she was used to hearing him. *The others have not learned to do so. Perhaps someday they will, but then again, most never learn such deep things. You have learned it well; you trust deeply. That's why you are the one leading the others. Jennifer, do you not yet understand who I am?*

"Simeon, you are my Shailma," she whispered.

Yes, Little One. I am he.

Somehow, Jennifer understood something she'd not understood before. Until now, she thought Simeon was merely a thought, something inside of herself. But now, and clearly it was Simeon himself who made this awareness come to her, she knew he was much more than that.

She had made her Shailma so small, so small indeed, when in fact, he was bigger than anything she could think of, or ponder, or consider, or understand. Her mind could not grasp just how big Simeon was. He knew all things; he was aware of all things; he was everywhere, at all times.

Jennifer had no need to fear or worry or be concerned, yet she was. The oddest of all was that Simeon knew his little one had found a new understanding of his bigness and that even though she was afraid, she would keep going; not because of who she was, but because of who he was. Suddenly that became enough for her, and she found her courage.

She heard Bella behind her. "Can we go this way?" she asked.

"I hope so, Auntie," Jennifer replied with a new confidence that no matter what, Simeon would get them to where they needed to be.

They jumped from open space to open space when the fire that was lapping at the ground would settle enough to let them pass. "I don't know where we are going, or when we are going to get there, or what we'll find once we get wherever it is we are getting to," Jennifer shouted back to the others, "but I'm assuming it will be the tablet."

Jennifer assumed right. The tablet *was* where they were going. Although, it was all the way on the other side of the Dark Land. It was a long way. The sun was on the downward part of its journey so it was questionable if they'd make it or not before the sun had set, or before the miserable king became impatient and gave a final shout for the land to collapse into itself, consuming all that was within its grasp.

It was getting harder and harder to see where to step because of the thickness of sulfur that was floating up. It was also getting harder and harder to breathe. The Travelers were trying to cover their faces; the sulfur was burning their eyes and making it hard to take a breath without choking.

"KEEP YOUR HEADS UP," Jennifer screamed behind her. It was nearly impossible to look up and look down at the same time. Nearly impossible, not altogether impossible.

Judah shouted back. "I DON'T KNOW IF THIS IS THE RIGHT WAY! IT'S TOO DANGEROUS!"

"THERE'S NO OTHER WAY," his sister shouted. "THIS IS THE ONLY WAY!"

All the while the Travelers were struggling to find the way, Bahlmish was getting frustrated because he couldn't seem to find any of the Nakahs and he didn't understand why King Shrailzhar had sent him. Bahlmish had always assumed the king knew where the Nakahs dwelt and he could have easily summoned them to come. Why he'd sent Bahlmish, the Chief Executive Sergeant couldn't figure out, unless he had given the king far too much credit and Shrailzhar didn't know as much about the land or have nearly as much power as Bahlmish had thought.

Regardless, the king had sent his Chief Executive Sergeant, and now he too was fearful. If he failed to bring back the Nakah Warriors, the king would certainly lift up his sword, and Bahlmish would lose his head. He looked harder and called louder. He hoped maybe one of those he'd brought with him was having better luck and wondered if they had already located some of the Nakah Warriors.

Just as Bahlmish was considering going back to where the king and the army were waiting, something caught the corner of his eye. He whipped his head around to see if he could figure out what it was. There—nearly invisible in the atmosphere—were the Nakahs. There were only a few, but those few would know where to find the others.

Bahlmish kicked his spiked boots into the sides of the dragon he sat upon. "HiYah!" he screamed and turned the black beast toward the cowering Nakahs. If anyone had been watching, they would have seen the dragon turned so sharply that Bahlmish nearly topped right off of the side. He hung on tighter. "HiYah!" he screamed again. He needed to hurry. If the Nakahs saw him coming, they may have sped up and become so hidden in the skies of Trilleah that Bahlmish might never find them again.

There were not many reasons for the Nakah Warriors to be called, but recently, they had been put on notice by King Shrailzhar. They knew fully that when the king called them, it would be for a vicious battle against the Shamar Shailmas. The Nakahs were brave enough, but even the strongest of Nakah Warriors did not wish to battle the Shamar Shailmas. After all, the Shamars were the only beings that dwelt in the atmosphere that had more power than the Nakahs.

If that battle began, likely the Nakah Warriors would lose many of their members. So, when King Shrailzhar put them on notice, they had hidden in the atmosphere. But those few who remained uncovered had been spotted, and now they were leading Bahlmish right to the place in the invisible realm where the rest were hiding ... trembling ... desperate not to be found.

This Present Darkness

12

Pierce let out a thunderous shout. Now, one might think that with so many loud bangs and shakings and booms and shrieks, the Travelers would be used to it and less easily startled. That was not the case. Pierce's loud shout did startle the others and Jennifer jumped, losing her balance. Judah had to leap back and grab her arm as she lunged forward, just to keep her from falling.

"PIERCE," Judah shouted angrily. "SHUT UP!" It wasn't like Judah to be unkind or rude, but he had watched his sister be pulled below the ground once already, so now seeing her nearly topple into a large crater in the ground was more than enough to make him angry.

"Why are you yelling, anyway?" he demanded.

"I'm sorry, I really am, but I caught a glimpse of something in the sky that I thought you all should see," Pierce replied. "It startled me!" He was at the end of the parade of Travelers, so he could see above the heads of the others. When he saw this thing that was hovering above them, Pierce decided they should all know about its presence, whether or not they decided to look for themselves.

Sam twisted his head up immediately, always interested in such things that might be hovering above him. Matt hesitated before whipping his head up toward the sky. From the last time he had looked back toward a commotion—and all that had happened when he did—he'd promised himself not to be so foolish again and so now, he sincerely did not want to look.

"Maybe it's better not to see all things," he whispered to Bella who was just ahead of him.

Jennifer, however, looked up immediately—as soon as she regained her balance, that is. Judah looked up but did not let go of his sister's arm. Matt even saw Bella look up, which surprised him since her eyes were still burning from the last time she looked at something in the sky. Some of the blood from earlier had dried on her face making her look quite wretched. Matt thought she was beautiful, nevertheless.

With everyone's heads tilted up and all eyes searching and finding nothing notable, Matt gave in and looked up. All he saw was a puncture in the sky which was getting bigger and bigger as bits were being torn away. It was getting to be dusk now, so it wasn't easy to see much of anything. The fact was that the sky was gray and dull … and without stars … and the moon was not yet beginning to share any of its light. Consequently, seeing was difficult.

"I don't see anything," Judah said sharply. He was still angry about being startled and had not yet let go of Jennifer; he probably wouldn't. Judah's memory whizzed back to the moment he saw the ground close over his sister; the look on her face was forever etched in his mind. The fire and the dragons he'd seen then, flashed in his mind now, as he tried for the thousandth time to erase it all.

Judah had been holding her hand only seconds before the vines had ripped her away that day and he was not about to let something so dreadful happen again now. He tightened his grip.

"Ouch, Judah," Jennifer winced and tried to pull away.

"Sorry," he whispered and loosened his grip slightly.

"I did see something," Pierce shot back. "It lifted up and disappeared into that gap in the sky," he explained. Nobody replied to him, but everyone set their eyes back to the ground and wondered where they might step next and where they should not step at all. Nobody paid any attention to what Pierce had said; perhaps they should have.

"I did see something," Pierce mumbled more to himself now, since it was clear that nobody was listening to him.

He saw something alright, and what he saw had not gone too far at all. It had not, in fact, disappeared into the gaps of the sky like Pierce had thought. What he'd seen remained very close. Nobody else could see it because it did not wish to be seen. In fact, it did not want even Pierce to see it, but it knew if it were only Pierce, it wouldn't matter too much; nobody would believe the boy anyway.

This thing had toiled for a long while and finally caused the Travelers to doubt Pierce quite thoroughly. This was all part of what needed to be done to give this "unseen thing" the power it required.

Yes, Pierce had a dark side, and even though the Travelers hadn't been able to give it a name or figure it out, they all knew it was there. He looked fine; there was nothing notable to give the bit of darkness away. Sure, he had jet black hair that was always covering much of his face in such a way as to give off a strangeness, and then there were those tattoos.

Some were on his arms, and there were a couple on his neck and even one beside his left eye. Most were pictures or words, but some were symbols that nobody ever asked him about. It wasn't because they weren't deeply curious about them, it was more because they were afraid of what they might mean. Sometimes, it's better not to know such things. They were undoubtedly harmless and just part of his dark style.

No, it was not even those tattoos that suggested darkness. Pierce had plugs in his ears and a ring in his lip but those things, too, were a part of Pierce's charm, not a part of the darkness. He did take a little getting used to, especially since the others were unused to one of such great differences. Pierce never tried to be something he wasn't, no matter who tried to fit him into their own mold.

"Don't judge a book by its cover," came to mind when the Travelers quietly talked about a new tattoo or another piercing he'd gotten between journeys. Pierce was just Pierce, and although he chose to have his appearance be different than the others, it was not those things that made any difference to the rest of the Travelers. It was something else altogether; something else none of them talked about, but they all pondered often.

Sure, he was painfully angry at Miriam—who wouldn't be? Of course, he wore the thick skin of guilt from losing Peter, but didn't all the Travelers share his feelings about their own loved ones who had been taken from them? They were all angry at somebody for something, were they not?

Indeed, it was not how Pierce looked that suggested darkness; nothing of this darkness that was hidden on the inside showed itself on the outside. Pierce himself, didn't even recognize it was there because it hid so well. In fact, the darkness that hid deep within his heart usually took great precaution to hide—even from him—the very one who carried it.

It was this very present darkness that Pierce had briefly seen. The reason none of the others had seen it was because it belonged to Pierce. He owned it. He had felt little bits of it, here and there, before Trilleah and more since he'd traveled to the Dark Land. But he had never seen it—at least, not with his eyes. Now that he had, though, he was unaware that it was something inside of himself that he'd seen slip out into the air.

Pierce shook his head. How did he see it and nobody else did? Were they even looking? Even more, he wondered why none of them believe that he'd seen something? Did they think he randomly made something up just to annoy them? Did they wonder if he was so crazy that he saw things that were not there? Even worse, did Judah think he'd shouted just to startle them? To add more fear? To cause harm to Jennifer?

Sure, Pierce and Jennifer had never really gotten along. Right from the very first meeting between the two, when Bella reamed Pierce out in front of the young girl, he and Jennifer were like sandpaper. But Pierce would never purposely put her—or anyone—in danger.

"That's simply ridiculous," he whispered to himself.

Bella was often angry with him for wandering away from the hollow or leaving the group behind, and she assumed it was because he was selfish or thoughtless. It never occurred to her—and she never bothered to ask him—that there may be another reason altogether. Now, of course, he had revealed that Miriam was the reason he'd done all those things that seemed at the time to Bella as selfish and thoughtless.

Now, he could let her know that Miriam had been there from the beginning and Pierce had only done what was necessary to keep her away from the Travelers. *She'll be sorry,* he thought to himself, *that she thought the worst of me when I was only trying to protect her.*

Of course, there were many times when he was jealous of Jennifer, and he never bothered to hide those feelings. *But then again, he reasoned, so was Bella.* He saw it. He had noticed before Jennifer came to Trilleah how Bella led the small troops with great pride. It was she who led them to find the first couple tablets, and she reminded them of it often.

Those first tablets were not hidden all that well, mind you. None had been plunged below the ground in an adder's pit. There weren't any that were tucked beneath a baby dragon with the angry fire-breathing Mamma so close by.

The first few that were found had only Pierce, Bella, and Matt to figure it all out. There wasn't much to figure, though. The maps were well laid out with very few hindrances. There was very little that Shrailzhar had set up to keep the tablets from being collected. Surely the king had thought those first few would not matter because the last few would never be found.

But then Bella brought Judah, and Sam's Shailma brought him as well, and the next tablet was just that much harder to locate. It was hidden in darkness and took a great effort from all of them to dig it up once it was found. The king had buried it on the side of the mountain, and it was indeed difficult to get out. But they did get it out. And there were very few creatures to get in their way.

Sure, they'd met with the cradle bugs a couple of times before, and Pierce had a good chunk of his flesh chewed off. But nothing like this! Nothing like the last few journeys. It was obvious the king had become concerned and had begun setting up elaborate and nearly impenetrable traps for them, such as the Labyrinth.

That's why Bella had finally agreed with the Shailmas to bring Jennifer. Once she came, even though she was highly annoying to Pierce from the beginning, it was clear that her presence was necessary. It had been clear to Pierce—even if none of the others had known it at the time—that there was something about Jennifer that was a key to finding the rest of the tablets.

Pierce had watched as the timid, frail little girl quickly took charge and Bella was forced to take a step—or many steps—back. She was no longer the leader and Pierce had noticed Bella become more and more jealous of this little one who had taken her place.

He may have had jealousy toward this little one, but Pierce's jealousy was minor compared to Bella's. No; it was certainly not jealousy which caused a certain darkness to reside in him.

Pierce looked ahead to Bella. He could see it in her face even now as she stumbled along. Jennifer and Judah were in front of her, and she walked alone behind them. Of course, she had quite a crush on Matt, who walked quietly behind her, but he hardly seemed to notice her most days. His attention was almost fully on breaking the curse and freeing the soul of his father.

Pierce tried to watch all the goings-on ahead of him for a time, which was difficult because of the careful attention that needed to be given to the ground.

There seemed to be fewer cracks and openings in the ground here, but the pillars of sulfur were rising just the same. It did feel like, at any moment—with just one small bump or gentle shake—the ground would simply give way and they would all plummet into the great abyss they knew was bubbling right below. Even if they could not see it right now, they knew it was there. Pierce's throbbing finger and their ruined lunch and hungry bellies reminded them of such things.

He watched Bella long enough to see an unmistakable look of rejection and jealousy in her eye as Judah grabbed onto Jennifer's arm instead of her own.

"She must feel so alone," Pierce whispered. He did have an eye for her as she was very beautiful, but Bella seemed to look right past Pierce, which only proved to frustrate him all the more.

And then, Pierce began a conversation in the depths of his soul. He didn't know it and assumed it was simply his deeply hidden jealous thoughts, but it was, in fact, a very real conversation with the dark presence which lingered in his heart. That presence wanted to make a home there, to be invited to stay. But for now, it was content to linger and be only a guest.

Think Quickly

13

Bahlmish was getting impatient. He'd been following those few Nakah Warriors that he'd noticed for a long while now, but they didn't seem to be leading him to the others. The longer he followed, the more concerned he was becoming that King Shrailzhar would be getting impatient. The king was to be greatly feared, to be sure, but when he became impatient, it was to be promised that someone would lose their head.

With every rumble of the land or flash of lightning in the sky, Bahlmish knew time was getting shorter and shorter for the land. More and more of his dreams were fading from his grasp. Oh, how he wanted to be beside the king in his final kingdom. He had been the Chief Guard in charge of Malleana Forest for over fifty years now and had done a splendid job of the task.

Not even one soul had been released from the forest, and the curse of the Trows remained solid. Besides that, the forest had gotten larger—much larger than Bahlmish had let himself ever consider …

"Surely," he boasted to his generals time and time again, "the great King Shrailzhar must be happy with me!" And every time he said those words, he thought to himself, *This time I must be right. This time the king will come and say I have done a wonderful job. This time he will notice and give me a special place in his kingdom. Surely I have earned my place beside his throne!* So far, that hadn't happened. The king hadn't rewarded him yet, but Bahlmish was still hopeful.

But now, much of his hope was fading since Bahlmish could not find the armies of the Nakah Warriors anywhere. He began to wonder if those few that had been seen were aware they were being followed and instead of hurrying straight back to the others, these few were leading Bahlmish on a wild goose chase. That had to be it.

Without any doubt, if Bahlmish did not return soon with the Nakah Warriors, King Shrailzhar would give the final order to destroy Trilleah and Bahlmish would find himself right in the midst of that destruction.

"HiYah!" he screamed and dug his steel-studded boots deeper into the side of the horrible dragon upon which he rode. The brood of vipers that made up the dragon's tail writhed and twisted greatly. They hissed and spat. Their fiery eyes were searching frantically for signs of any Nakah Warriors as well as keeping eyes on the Travelers.

The vipers were having more and more difficulty seeing those ones for whom they were searching, though, because of the vast number of Shamar Shailmas that were continuing to come and cover the Travelers. It would not be long before the Travelers would be impossible to see—even to the dragons' vipers.

Surely, those Shamar Shailmas were anticipating what was happening in the atmosphere. They were closely watching Bahlmish and the others as they continued their search for the Nakah Warriors.

"Pierce," Bella hollered just loud enough to be heard by the one she was calling. "Why are you lagging so far behind?"

Nobody else had even noticed, but Bella had been keeping an eye on each of the Travelers. She felt like a mother hen and a tad responsible for the well-being of each and every Traveler.

Ever since her own mother had passed on when she was so young, she'd watched her older sister, Molly, fill in the role of "mother" to her. Then, when Molly had the twins, Bella watched another transformation of her older sister as she learned to be a mother to two babies. Bella had learned so much from her dear sister, and she missed her greatly.

When Molly and Theo had been in that horrible accident, Bella was instantly thrown into the role of mother. She wasn't asked about it or consulted whatsoever; she was given no time to consider the role. It just became hers, overnight.

Bella had been so young herself; there was no option, though, since the twins had no other family to look after them. Now Bella sort of mothered everyone, especially here in Trilleah, since she was the oldest girl. Consequently, since she'd noticed Pierce falling farther and farther behind the group, she made a point of keeping her eye on him. It was a good thing too, because now he was a long way behind and she was curious—and concerned—about it.

Pierce didn't answer her right away because he was deeply involved in a conversation he was having in his mind. He didn't notice she'd been calling to him.

"I really can't believe she is leading anybody anywhere," Pierce mumbled to himself.

I know ... she is young and inexperienced and foolish really. That one is foolish to think she knows much of anything. He responded in his mind to his own mumbling, and the conversation carried on. Some words he mumbled to himself under his breath and some thoughts he kept hidden in his mind.

Pierce was surprised at the conversation he was having with himself because just last night he had felt bad for her. Less than twenty-four hours ago, Pierce and Jennifer had sat on the shore and watched Leviathan disappear under the bloodied waters. They sat huddled together; he had tucked her under his arm, and they had sobbed for a long while.

But now, from somewhere, all these feelings were being stirred up and he was becoming more and more agitated with the thoughts he was having about Jennifer.

Of course, it was not himself with whom he was having the conversation, but he was unaware of that. The truth was, in fact, that the conversation he thought he was having with his mind was really being had with the darkness which was rising within him. For a long time, he went back and forth with his thoughts. He felt sad for the frail young girl who had her parents taken from her so early. *And now, for some reason, she has been put in charge of all this*, he thought.

"I'm sure she did not ask for any of this," he mumbled. But then as he would be feeling bad for her, deep thoughts of anger would take over and he would become enraged with jealousy at her place at the front, as the leader.

It wasn't as if he wanted that place—not really—for it must be so very difficult. It was more like he thought he could do a better job of it. Pierce had no idea how much time that one whom he saw as weak and frail, spent with her Shailma. He had no clue what Simeon had asked of her, and he certainly had no way of knowing she was willing to follow him and be obedient to anything her Shailma asked of her, no matter how big … or how small.

That was the key, but it was a key Pierce did not have, and so, he was angry. He could have held that same key as Jennifer held, but it was a heavy one. It required a complete surrender of will and desire, and a complete trust in something unseen—both of which Pierce could not do.

Pierce would not believe even when Jennifer and Bella told him what they were seeing. He refused! "I will not believe unless I can see it for myself," he had shouted. And so, because of such doubt, he could never carry the key that Jennifer had.

In fact, it was that very refusal to believe in his Shailma and all he could not see that allowed for this darkness to come to Pierce in the first place. That darkness was now telling him he *should* be angry with Jennifer. *I have every right, after all*, he thought. *I was here first—long before that girl even knew Trilleah existed. I should be in charge, not her!* And his thoughts rattled on; as the darkness poured fuel on the sparks that were already there, Pierce became caught in a trap of his own making brought on from jealousy and unbelief.

Jennifer had been right earlier, when she reacted so loudly and with great trepidation to Pierce's declaration of not believing. She didn't fully understand the importance of it but understand or not, she knew his words were dangerous. Now with the vicious battle going on in Pierce's mind for control of his thoughts, it was apparent that once again—and even though she did not yet know it—Jennifer had been right.

"PIERCE," Bella called louder. Her curiosity for the one who was getting farther and farther behind had now turned to concern. "PIERCE!" she screamed, for by now he was lagging a far distance behind.

Her voice finally reached his ears and he looked up, startled. He had not realized he'd fallen so far behind and became panicky when he saw there was so much distance between him and the rest of the Curse Breakers.

"Pierce, pay attention," he mumbled.

He shook his head and looked down at his burned finger. It was throbbing greatly by this time, and he wished he had not been so cocky as to have poked at the ground earlier. He was just trying to make a point to the others that Jennifer didn't know as much as she was trying to get them to believe. However, as his finger was swollen and terribly blistered, he wondered—just for a second—if maybe she did.

Maybe he should start believing her like the others seemed to, but the thought barely had time to reach his brain before other thoughts —nasty thoughts—moved in and crowded the first one out.

He moved his feet quickly. He may have been angry and jealous and refusing to acknowledge that Jennifer was wiser than himself, but he did not want to get left behind. Nobody would slow much, so he had to hurry. He quickened his steps and it didn't take long for him to catch up to the rest. Bella saw he was near now and whispered to him.

"Pierce, come up here with me," she said and waved him toward her.

He was not about to miss the chance to be near Bella, so he skipped ahead of Sam and Matt and the others who seemed less than pleased to have to move over for him to get by. Nevertheless, they did move over because they didn't want to get knocked over ... Pierce was unpredictable enough to do a thing just so dreadful.

Once Pierce got himself to where Bella was carefully tiptoeing this way and that, he immediately wished he had stayed far behind. He thought she wanted him to be near for her safety or to give her some sense of security. It turned out he was wrong. That was not why she wanted him beside her; not at all.

"Why are you lagging so far behind?" she asked. It seemed the reason she wanted him close was to reprimand him for this and lecture him about that. Pierce pretended he didn't know what she was talking about and hoped she'd drop the lecture. He tried to change the subject and take her mind elsewhere, but she was not going to be easily persuaded. Distracting Bella didn't seem to be an option.

"Pierce, who were you talking to back there?" she asked. As she did, Bella stopped briefly and turned to him; just for a split second. She looked him in the eye and saw something looking back at her that was most certainly not Pierce.

"Pierce, what's going on?" Bella demanded. She was not happy to see that something dark was going on with her friend.

"I don't know what you're talking about." He shrugged his shoulders and turned to keep walking. "We've got to keep going," he muttered.

He didn't realize that something dark had gotten into his mind which was now masking what he heard, what he saw, and what he said. It was like an invisible filter had been placed around his mind and everything that was going out—or coming in—had to go through the filter. The only way the darkness could remain, was if it hid from the owner of the mind, which in this case was Pierce and so, it worked hard to remain hidden.

It couldn't hide from Bella, though, she had seen it. She knew what it was and she also knew there was only one way to get rid of it … but she had to be careful. Pierce was unpredictable by his very nature, and so if Bella worked too hard or too quickly to make him aware of the darkness that had moved into his mind, she'd be vulnerable to the unpredictability and might end up in grave danger.

Be very cautious, Bella, she heard Shura whisper. *Very careful. Do not move on this without my leading. Wait for me. There will be a perfect time to deal with this darkness but wait until I show you. If you panic or move without my direction, that darkness may invite more darkness in and then instead of dealing with a small enemy, you'll be doing battle against an army of darkness.*

"Oh dear," she said. Bella didn't realize she'd said it out loud, though.

"Oh dear?" Pierce asked. "Oh dear, what?"

Now she had to think quickly. Oh, how she wished she could keep her tongue from letting out those things that should remain in her mind. There were just times she could not seem to control her tongue, though, and every time it caused her trouble.

Think quickly, she told herself.

Summoned to War

14

"Finally," Bahlmish screeched. He had followed the few wandering Nakahs long enough, and they had finally led him to the den where their army was hiding from the king.

Bahlmish stayed a short distance away while he summoned the other six of the king's Major Generals to come and help him. It took no time at all for the others to reach Bahlmish and once they were all there —seven in all—they stormed the Nakahs' hiding place.

"Now hear this all Nakah Warriors, big and small, young and old. Listen to the orders of your king," Bahlmish bellowed. He would have chuckled as he watched the warriors fill with great fear and the enormous beings begin to tremble, if only he had a sense of humor or any ability within him to feel such things. He did not, however, have any such abilities and so he continued screaming his demands.

"The great and mighty King Shrailzhar has sent me to summon you to war!" It only took two moments for every single Nakah Warrior to come out from their place of hiding and stand in a war formation before Bahlmish. They had no use for this one who was screaming such orders at them, but they knew if they disregarded his commands, the king would come after them and destroy every last one of them in the most dreadful of ways.

"The king is waiting for you now on the flatlands south of the shoreline of the sea."

None of them moved. Bahlmish shook his head in disgust at the stupidity of these ones who were supposed to have the power to overtake and defeat the Shamar Shailmas.

The vipers that were woven into the tails of the Major Generals' beasts snapped and spit and snarled, for they were ravenous and disgusting creatures. Even though they hated with great hatred the Shamar Shailmas, these vipers would gouge out the eyes of anything that came near—the Nakah Warriors included.

"What are you waiting for?" Bahlmish demanded. "Go to the king NOW you dull-witted imbeciles!" He looked to the other Major Generals and fumed at the ignorance of ones such as these Nakahs.

"GO NOW!" he screamed again at the Nakahs. And to the Major Generals, he shouted, "go with these ones who are completely without sense and make sure they get to the king. If these do not make it in all their numbers to King Shrailzhar, you will lose your heads to my very own sword!"

With the orders now given, Bahlmish stepped back. He watched and he counted as the Nakah Warriors swarmed swiftly from their hiding places. There were 49,497 in all. He watched as the six Major Generals flew just behind the Nakah Warriors in the direction of the king who would most certainly be impatient and raging with anger by this time.

If the king did not bring his sword down on the Major Generals' heads, Bahlmish would be surprised. "As long as they get those idiots to the king, I don't care if they keep their heads or they roll into the sea!" he whispered to the vipers.

The Travelers turned their faces to the sky; there was no doubt that something drastic was going on in the atmosphere. The air above them was swirling viciously, and although their eyes couldn't see it, they felt it without a doubt. Even though the dim sun was well on its way to hiding behind the broken-down horizon, the sky unusually turned three or four shades darker in an instant. Bella looked toward the sun and saw it was the same. Jennifer looked in front of them, but nothing had changed there either.

It was definitely in the sky where something was going on, just not in any place where they could see. Whatever was happening, it was out of the realm of their sight. The motion was, without a doubt, behind the veil of the atmosphere where their eyes could not see unless opened by a Shailma. That was not happening, and so, while none of the Travelers could see what was going on; there was no doubt something was.

"What's happening?" Kaija Mae was the first to speak and acknowledge what everyone else was too afraid to acknowledge.

"I don't know," whispered one in a voice of unbridled terror.

"Where can we hide?" pleaded another.

"There is nowhere to hide," screeched a third.

Jennifer, however, remained quiet. Well, on the outside, she remained quiet. Inside she was panicking greatly, and desperately begging Simeon to come and give some help.

Simeon, she whispered for she was much too afraid to shout—even in the silences of her mind. *What's happening, Simeon? Where are you? I need your help! Simeon? Simeon!!*

This was her typical practice when any fear-stirring dilemma showed itself. Even though Simeon had told her, again and again, to remain calm, that he could not be heard if she let her mind become filled with anxiousness, Jennifer continued to react in the same way.

Finally, after she'd panicked long enough and had become so desperate to hear her Shailma that she quieted herself down, Simeon came to her. What he said was not surprising, although, it was annoying because Jennifer did not think there was adequate time for a lecture right at the moment. Certainly, it could wait for later.

A lecture came anyway. Even though it was short, and one Jennifer had heard a thousand times before, she vowed to try harder to remember it for next time. She waited with growing impatience as her Shailma reminded her to hush and remain calm in her mind. When it seemed he was finished reminding her of all the things she'd surely forget immediately, Jennifer spoke.

Simeon, she begged. *What's going on? The air is moving and not from a typical Trilleah wind either. It seems like there is a whirlwind or dark force above us. Are we going to be sucked up into it?*

Oh, Little One, no. You are not going to be taken from this land; not yet. But you are right. There is a whirlwind above you, in the atmosphere. And then, as Jennifer tried to remain calm as she'd just been sharply reminded, she listened ever so carefully as Simeon explained what was going on.

As the rest of the Travelers whispered to their Shailmas, and their heads continued being turned toward the sky looking for whatever it was that was stirring up the atmosphere, Jennifer focused all her attention on two things; listening to Simeon and walking carefully on the fragile ground.

She learned of the Nakah Warriors and that the king was going to try and launch the "War of the Firmament," as Simeon called it.

But Simeon, she wailed, *I don't even know what a firmament is. How can it be in a war?*

Dear Little One, Simeon calmed her, *it is the atmosphere—that place that is there but unseen by the eyes. It is the air far above you, where you feel the stirring beginning now. This is the firmament, and this is where the war will be waged.*

Jennifer was trying to stay calm, really she was, but when one is told that war is about to break out in a place that is unseen yet so close and felt whether seen or not, and against an army that is dangerous and not visible, calmness can be awfully difficult to find. She searched hard for even a crumb of it but found none.

Jennifer let out a horrible wail.

It was not so much that her own life seemed about to be snuffed out, but more because all they had worked for and seen and walked through and experienced was about to be for no reason at all. Wasted. It was the thought that if Jennifer's life were to be lost, then all of those cursed souls would be lost as well as those who were behind her now. Judah and Bella, Kaija Mae and Aviel, Matt, and Sam and Pierce, and all the others she'd come to love deeply.

Oh, all those who Jennifer had seen in the adder's pit suddenly came to her mind. Those precious ones who had called to her begging for help—for redemption. Justice, Sam's sweet little sister, would be lost. She would spend every day of forever tormented and anguished and … oh, Jennifer could not let herself think about the loss. She tried, oh, how desperately she tried.

Of course, she did not particularly *want* to have her life taken —the breath removed from her lungs—but that was not what weighed the heaviest on her soul. It was not her life she wanted to save; she'd settled in her belly a long time ago that if her life was the price required to save her mamma's soul from the terrible eternal curse of the Trows, then that was the price she would pay. Now it seemed the cost would be much greater than she'd ever considered … a price she'd never agreed to pay was being demanded of her now.

Was there another option?

Could she demand her Shailma take her home? Could she refuse to carry on with this journey? It seemed to be her very purpose for existing—but perhaps she could settle for less than this. Surely she could learn to be happy back in Westlock and forget any of this had ever happened. Certainly, she could get over the loss of Mamma and Daddy. Mamma would understand, wouldn't she?

All the while she was so busy being alarmed in her belly and hysterical in her mind, Simeon was trying without success to get her attention. Sometimes it was a wonder that Simeon himself did not abandon her to her fear, but he was a Shailma, after all, and Shailmas never leave their own. There was not one thing Jennifer could do or think or not do or not think that would cause Simeon to leave her and so even now, in the very depths or her craziness, the Shailma remained.

A noise disturbed her ranting—not a loud noise but a noise nonetheless. She looked over and saw that Sam had come up beside her and was calling her name.

"Jenny," he said for the umpteenth time and tapped her on the arm. Finally, he got her attention. "What's going on?" he whispered. "Do you know?" He was such a tall boy, but so young and naive and trusting. Sam trusted her. She didn't understand why, but it was obvious that he did.

Jennifer wanted to scream at him, to lash out and demand to know what made him think she'd know? Why did everyone think she would have the answers? But the truth was that she did know. Simeon had told her. He had not told her much, but enough that she knew a War in the Firmament was brewing.

As she tried to explain to Sam what a firmament was and what she'd heard from Simeon, she realized that she had not finished listening to her Shailma. She realized that once again she had heard only a small bit of his words and gone off on a crazy fearful rant so deep that Simeon had to step back or get hit with the debris of all her horribly fearful thoughts.

She wanted to go back and apologize to the Shailma—again— and ask for more information, but it was too late for now. Sam was there and he had a hundred questions of his own, most of which Jennifer had no answers to.

Oh, how Jennifer wished she'd never gone to the adder's pit and had never seen the feeble shadowy bodies of the Waiting Ones. But she had. She had heard the quiet but terrified cries of Justice and the deep, fearful voice of Tom, and the painful shrieks of Mamma. She was powerless to go back and change it—but it had indeed changed her.

Jennifer's cry of, *Oh, Mamma,* had turned into a cry for all of the Waiting Ones, for indeed she had seen the horror of their eternities unless she and the others could find that last tablet and break the curse that held them. But now, with the War of the Firmament stirring and getting ready to begin, the grains of sand running through the hourglass were nearly gone. The Travelers must do whatever they came to do before that trumpet could blast, signaling the start of the unseen war in the heavenlies.

Jennifer felt a new bravery like she'd never felt before come upon her—a warrior bravery—and quite unexpectedly Simeon's words echoed in her mind.

"You are a Princess Warrior, Little One," he had said to her not so long ago, and in one brief moment, she understood that indeed, she was.

Fear Unchallenged

15

"Please, we've got to hurry," Jennifer wailed. She didn't care any longer who—or what—might hear her because they were surrounded by the Shailmas and therefore, protected—for now, at least. She didn't know how long that protection would last, though, and panic was settling in.

With the War of the Firmament beginning, Jennifer had no way of knowing how many of the Shailmas surrounding them would have to leave, and she didn't want to think about it. Simeon had said there would be enough remaining with them that she didn't have to be concerned—she was trying hard not to be.

So there they were. Jennifer, who was by far the smallest and frailest of them all, was leading them quickly over precarious ground which was mostly covered with thick billows of sulfur and smoke. It was hard to see the ground and the dimness that had set into the land offered no help whatsoever.

When one step would find soft ground, her foot would quickly move until it found a section that was still firm. It was long and tedious and tiring. Her legs were sore, and they should have been. Everyone's legs were tired and sore and they were about ready to collapse.

The Travelers hadn't sat or taken a rest since they left the hollow early this morning. Even when they ate the morsels of food that hadn't burned up, they stood because the ground was too dangerous to sit on. Pierce's finger was proof of that and a constant reminder of just how important it was that they stayed upright with only their feet touching the ground. They weren't sure if the insulated pads which they couldn't see would hold anything more than their feet; none of them wanted to find out.

It was even more awkward for Jennifer to try to maneuver such unpredictable ground with Judah holding onto her so tightly. She had tried to loosen his grip and had asked him more than once not to hold on so tightly, but every time he said the same thing.

"I won't lose you again, Jelly Bean."

And so it was. He held on tightly, she wiggled to try and find a less pinched position for her hand, and together the twins walked an uncertain and risky road.

Right behind the twins were Bella and Pierce. The twins couldn't hear for sure what they were saying or talking about, but there was no doubt the two of them were bickering about something unimportant. Once, the twins heard their auntie Bella ask Pierce about something in his eye, which seemed innocent enough, but his reaction was loud and angry.

"I have no idea what you're talking about!" he'd answered.

So, on and on they bickered, back and forth, arguing and whispering—whispering and arguing—but holding tightly to one another all the same.

Next in line was Sam. He had moved back between Bella and Matt because that was where he felt the safest. He'd heard far too much information from Jennifer, and none of it sat well in his mind or his belly. Her explanations had made him nervous so this seemed like the best place for him to be.

Pierce was never particularly kind to Sam, especially with his outrageous red hair which Bella thought was fantastic and told him so regularly. Maybe that was why Pierce was so mean to Sam. Maybe he was jealous. He seemed to be jealous a lot, especially of anything or anyone that took Bella's attention from him. He had an outrageous crush on the beautiful blonde-haired girl and made no attempt to hide it from anyone—especially Bella.

Matt and Kaija Mae were behind Sam, and as usual, Matt was chattering away quietly, trying to keep everyone around him from being afraid. He hid the fact that his own fear was bubbling within him—as he always did. Jennifer used to think Matt didn't feel fear; that he was somehow immune to it. But since meeting his father, Tom, in the adder's pit, she knew differently. It seemed like Matt was a lot like his father, and Jennifer didn't know him, but somehow in that pit, she knew things she'd not known before. It was as though seeing all that she saw somehow gave her knowledge she'd otherwise not have had.

The rest of the Travelers were even further behind them. Aviel had been friendly here and there but didn't mingle much with the others —not that this was any time to mingle. There were some others and Jennifer knew some of their names, but couldn't remember them now.

None of them had made much of an effort to communicate or get to know anyone else; they stayed mostly to themselves, which was perfectly fine with Jennifer and Judah. They had enough to concern themselves with already and didn't need anyone else adding to the heaviness of the burden of leading this group to the last tablet.

Jennifer didn't need anyone else asking questions to which she had no answers, and for sure, she already had enough Travelers arguing with her over every little thing. *Yes, let them stick to themselves*, she thought.

The skies were thundering now, and an entire storm of lightning was being thrown around, lighting up the sky. It was eerie. The lightning was not going from the sky to the ground like it would back home. It was going more from one side of the sky to the other and back again—like the Nephilim were playing tennis with the massive bolts of fiery lightning sending them back and forth. Jennifer let her mind imagine such a sight for a moment.

Besides thunder and lightning, they could hear sounds coming from what Jennifer could only assume was the Nakah Warriors.

The air was filled with whirring noises. It sounded as though the entire sky was spinning like a carnival ride. Faster and faster it went, and while they couldn't see it, they could hear it, and it sounded furious. For a time they had to plug their ears. There were also the sounds of, well, nobody really could tell what it was the sounds of. Sam said it sounded like back home when his dad would round up the cattle and their hooves would all stampede hard on the ground. Maybe that's what it was. Maybe it was the sound of all the dragons that the Nakahs sat upon stampeding toward the Shamar Warriors. Maybe the great war really was about to begin.

Jennifer began telling Judah about all that Simeon had told her. She spoke about the war that was coming and how maybe this sound was just that. He listened carefully to every word she spoke. Now and then he'd interrupt to ask a question … to which she did not know the answer. After about seven or eight of those questions, she realized she needed more information … a lot more.

"I don't know," she whined. "I don't know any of it."

Simeon, she searched in her mind for the only one who had the answers. *Will we be able to see the war? Will we know it's going on? Is it going on now? How will we know, Simeon? How will we know?*

One question at a time, Little One, she heard come back to her. So one question at a time it would be.

Simeon, she asked. *Is the war going on now?*

Oh no, not yet, Jenny. And with that one question, Simeon went on to answer a multitude of other ones yet unasked.

You will be able to see much of the war because your cloud of Shamar Shailmas will be occupied fighting and will be unable to cover you as much as they are now. You will not be completely uncovered, though, for some will stay to protect the Travelers. However, many of the Shailmas will undoubtedly be forced to fight the Nakah Warriors, so you will be able to see much more than you should, I'm sad to say.

You must decide before any of that, though, Jenny, and tell the others as well, to be unafraid. You must decide. No matter what happens, no matter what you see or how you feel, you must keep going. You must carry on. The tablet is near, and you must find it and add it to the others while the king is preoccupied with the war. You must find it, Little One. You must find it ...

King Shrailzhar is not wise at all, the Shailma continued. *He thinks he is, oh yes, he thinks he is the wisest king of all time. He is so wrong ...* Simeon laughed. *He does not realize that while the war is going on, everything else continues as well. He has not even considered such things.*

The land will continue to shake, you will continue to move toward the tablet, your Shailmas will remain with you since we are not Shamar Shailmas. That will be your opportunity to sneak to wherever you need to go and retrieve the final tablet. The king is causing his own distractions and he doesn't even realize it.

You are nearly there, Little One, but it will be a war for you as well because there will be much fear. That is where your battle will be fought—in your soul and in your mind. You must keep control of your thoughts at all times; that is where you will either win or lose the battle. If fear overtakes you—if you allow such a thing—then you will not go to the end ... you will quit. Fear will win. You must control your thoughts or they will control you.

That sounded familiar; Jennifer was certain that Simeon had told her that before, but when? She tried to find it in her memory but couldn't locate it. Regardless, she knew she'd heard it before.

"Fear is a terrible thing," she said to her brother who continued to crowd her.

"It is?" he asked and seemed surprised at such an idea—like he'd never thought about it before. "I sometimes think fear is our friend —like it makes us aware of things we need to stay away from."

"I suppose," she muttered. It dawned on her that she'd never really thought about it too deeply herself. Judah seemed to make a very good point. So, for the next little bit, while listening to the whirring of the air and waiting for her eyes to begin seeing bits and pieces of the war that would certainly be happening any time now, she pondered fear.

Maybe it has some good in it, she finally decided. Simeon butted in straightaway, even though Jennifer had not wanted him to nor looked for him or even considered asking him about it.

"Little One," he whispered to her, "it depends what you are fearing, whether it is good or bad. Sometimes, you can fear a good thing and miss an opportunity." That made sense to her, she supposed.

"Other times," he continued, "you may not fear something you should and be in grave danger." Simeon was referring to Pierce right at the moment, but because Jennifer had not yet become aware that a darkness had presented itself to Pierce; she didn't realize Simeon was being specific about him.

But later, when Pierce would begin to pose a danger to her and the others, this thought of Simeon's would return and she would understand it completely.

Something flashed in the sky just above the twins, pulling Jennifer's attention away from Simeon. She looked to Judah to see if he'd noticed it and from the look on his face, he had.

"Did you see that?" he asked her.

"Yes," she whispered. Jennifer squeezed his hand and said desperately, "don't let go of me, Judah."

"No chance, Jelly Bean," he replied. "No chance."

Again, something caught their eyes. Now Bella noticed and gasped loudly. "What was that?" she squealed.

"I don't know," both Judah and Jennifer blurted out at the same time. Pierce had Bella by the arm already and pulled her closer to him. They had to be so careful. Even though they wanted to break into a fast run and get to where they needed to be—wherever that might be— the ground was too unsteady, too weak, and too unpredictable to do such a thing. They had to keep their feet from moving so fast that they'd lose their balance, while also keep their wits about them—a difficult conundrum, to be sure.

This way, Jennifer heard Simeon call. She felt a tug to the left of her which was odd since Judah was on her right.

East? she asked silently.

Yes, Jennifer, east. Move ... NOW.

She moved now.

"This way," she whispered over her shoulder. It had gotten quite dark, and the only light was from the flashes of lightning that continued to be tossed through the air, back and forth. She hoped the others would see the ones in front of them and follow. There was no time for anyone to get lost.

Unfortunately, NOT everybody could see and unfortunately, some DID get lost. Everyone, in fact, except the twins. Nobody had seen Judah and Jennifer turn to the east, so when Bella and Pierce went straight, so did everyone else.

The rumblings in the sky were so loud that nobody heard Jennifer say they were turning east and the twins could not hear that no one stayed behind them when they did turn out. As soon as the twins arrived to where Simeon had led them, they turned around to pull the others inside the empty crevice they'd found on the side of the hill.

No one was behind them. No one was in front of them. The twins were alone. Judah looked at his sister and she looked right back to Judah. Neither spoke any words, but each knew exactly what the other was thinking.

The Battle Begins

16

King Shrailzhar had waited long enough, and now, with his patience depleted, he was furious … outraged … one might even say he was hysterically ravaged. His armies could not seize the Travelers until the Nakah Warriors came to take out a large number of the Shamar Shailmas. That was going to be difficult, but not impossible.

How badly he wanted those Travelers' souls. He hated them from the very second they had entered his land—especially that pernicious pair of twins. It seemed there was no trap he could set that would capture them and no fear big enough to make them stay away. Shrailzhar was unable, even though he tried time after time, to find their precious hollow after that one and only time his army had been able to surround it, and even when he sent armies to their home in Westlock or posted Nakahs at the Solstice gates, they still managed to slip into Trilleah.

Those Elliot twins were destroying his land, and now he was anxious to destroy them. They were the ones to blame for Trilleah's falling apart, and now, they would pay. Thinking of all these things enraged the king even more, but he felt their end was near and he was getting impatient waiting for those Nakah Warriors. They were his ticket to finally ending the journey of each and every one of those wretched Travelers.

Shrailzhar, who had finally reached the very end of his patience and was about to destroy another third of his army, finally heard a ruckus in the atmosphere. He turned to see that a great number of Nakahs were heading toward him. He shouted some angry remnants of outrage, and the land rumbled. If Trilleah lasted long enough for the battle to begin, it would be a miracle, for it was becoming weak at the seams from all the shaking and tearing.

"Finally!" the king roared to the Nakahs.

"Quickly," he commanded the army of 49,497 warriors who were lingering in the air and waiting for instructions from Shrailzhar. "You must destroy the Shamar Shailmas. I don't care what you do with them, just get them away from those Travelers!" The king didn't even consider that the Shamar Shailmas could hear him; perhaps he didn't know they could. Perhaps he didn't care.

The Shamars were no longer close to where the Army of Shrailzhar—and the king himself—had been waiting so maybe the king didn't realize the Shamars could hear him, no matter where they lingered.

It made no difference either way; the Shamar Shailmas were great in number and they stood on guard; ready. Ready to battle whatever came their way. Nothing would get past them. Nothing would capture the Travelers—not even one of them—for the Shamars were on guard, ready to fight.

And fight they would. The War of the Firmament was about to begin—the king was finally ready to send 45,000 of the Nakah Warriors out. The remaining 4,497 he would keep back for his own protection, just in case any of the Shamars broke through the front lines and came after the king. He wanted to be sure the Shamars could not reach him.

As the Nakah Warriors waited for their final instructions, they turned toward the Shamar Shailmas who were already in attack formation. As soon as they turned, a great and horrible ruckus broke out in the air. The winds picked up and ripped through the land, blowing the smoke and the sulfur every which way. The winds picked up embers that were still smoldering in the woodlands where the Travelers had been earlier, and deposited them throughout the land, some here and some there.

The embers that fell into the sea were extinguished. The embers that landed on the sand were blown about until the wind buried them beneath the sand. But the embers that were blown into the grasses and the tall weeds lit up instantly, causing fires to ignite all over the Dark Land.

The twins were somewhat safe inside the etched-out hideaway in the hill that Simeon had directed them to, but they were gravely panicked about where the others had gotten to.

"Judah," Jennifer cried. "Where are they? We've got to find them!" She was so distraught that she was not even noticing the enormous fireballs being hurled toward the hills.

"Jennifer, we CANNOT go out there!" He had to be brave for both of them; certainly, if he let the dread out that was rising within him, his sister would collapse, leaving him in an even worse predicament. If they had to get away quickly, he wouldn't be able to carry her so for now, and as hard as it was, he forced himself to keep calm—for Jennifer.

Judah swallowed hard. "The others will find a place to go while this battle rages. Don't forget, Jelly Bean," he shouted, "they have very wise Shailmas."

"I suppose," his sister sobbed.

"Jennifer, when they have YOU to lead them and YOU to seek Simeon, they get lazy—as do I. When YOU do all the work, we don't have to." Honestly, Judah didn't know where this was coming from because he'd certainly never considered any of it before. But now that he was considering it, he realized how true it was, and in the quietness of his mind, he whispered, *Shemaiah, I am sorry I've been so lazy and not sought you more.*

"They will find their Shailmas and learn a little more trust themselves! Jelly Bean, they'll be okay." Judah wanted to believe all that he was spouting—he really did—but right now it was more important that Jennifer believed it. *I think she's buying it,* he thought to himself, and by all indications, it seemed she was.

Jennifer sniffled a few times and wiped her eyes on her sleeve. "I miss them," she whimpered. That was not something she considered would be her feelings and it surprised her that it was. "We've been through so much, and now I'm scared for them." Judah could see she was getting herself worked up again, so he interrupted quickly and changed the subject.

"We have one tablet left to find, Jennifer—ONE! Can you believe that?" He began doing a little dance which looked utterly foolish, but it made her giggle, which was the purpose. There certainly was nothing within the boy that made him want to dance other than the love for his Jelly Bean!

There was a narrow rock ledge on the side of this hill, and Judah spit on it to see if it was bubbling underneath or if it was safe to rest on. The blob of his saliva just sat there in a puddle so he carefully and quickly touched his pinky to the rock. Still nothing. He touched it a little longer, and still, no feeling of heat wormed through his skin.

Judah took a twig that was hanging just outside and wiped off the rock.

"Sit for a while, Jenny," he said.

She did.

He sat beside her and put his arm around his frantic sister, pulling her close to him. The tiredness from Judah's not sleeping last night was beginning to get to him, and he laid his head against the side of the hill.

And there they sat—the two Travelers—alone in a dug-out hole in the side of a hill that was hidden behind some extraordinarily large bushes. They would never have found it if Simeon hadn't led Jennifer straight to it. They watched the lightning whip across the sky and talked about how strange it was that it never came down to the ground.

Back home the two of them would often sit and watch lightning storms together; Bella would make cocoa or sweet tea. But now, it was just Jennifer and Judah. There was no sweet tea, no hot cocoa, no Auntie Bella. Not here. Not now.

"Judah," Jennifer whispered with a quivering voice. A few tears hovering in the corners of her eyes begged to spill out. "Do you think we'll see Bella again?" Her voice cracked, but she sniffled and refused to let the tears fall.

"Of course we will, Jelly Bean," he assured her. "I bet she's sitting in a hole just like this one very close to here. I bet," he whispered, and even as he said the words his heart begged it to be true. "If we listen closely, we'll hear the sweet songs of Kaija Mae."

"Okay," Jenifer sulked. They began to listen harder than they'd ever listened for anything before.

Kaija Mae was singing alright, but far, far away from where the twins were tucked away. She was singing loudly, but none of the Travelers would hear this song … not tonight. They were lost and had not yet found any safe place to hide from all that was raging in the air.

Sam wanted to run, but Pierce and Matt held him back. He was having trouble catching his breath and had nearly gotten hit by a fireball. There were many of them flying through the air now. The wind was hurling the burning debris this way and that, and the Travelers had to watch every direction at all times to avoid getting hit with them.

When one of the larger fireballs came hurling right toward Sam, Matt was the one who'd seen it first and pulled Sam out of the way. Of course, they also had to be very careful not to lose their balance because the ground beneath was dangerously hot. Every once in awhile, before these wild winds had begun to rage, the Travelers thought they could hear the Sea of Acheron raging. It was eerie. They could hear it as though it was right there, but no matter where they looked, they could not see it … not yet anyway.

Since that wind had been stirred up, they could hear nothing other than its howling and screaming.

No; Sam was not doing okay at all and the others were trying to help him but were not successful at that task whatsoever.

"We have GOT to find shelter!" Pierce screamed against the wind. Nobody heard his wails, however, because the wind came and stole his words before they could reach anyone's ears.

Ashes flew at his face and he spit, already having a mouthful of sulfur and smoke. He cringed as his saliva sizzled on the ground and instantly burned up.

There was so much smoke being stirred in the air that it was getting more and more difficult to breathe. The Travelers had to find things to cover their noses and mouths with so the smoke didn't burn into their lungs. The sun had set long ago, but it was no longer dark in the land. Small fires were burning here and there, and the lightning that continued hurling across the sky provided more light than the Travelers were used to … or comfortable with.

Of all the days they'd spent in Trilleah in half-light or almost no light, and of all the terrifyingly deplorable things they had seen, now was the worst of it all by far. On the one day they wished they could see nothing at all, Trilleah was lit up for them to see everything there was to see. None of it was good.

"What has stirred up these winds?" Kaija Mae screamed. She didn't think anybody knew, but it never hurt to ask. Even if someone did know, the chances were high that the winds were not reacting to anything good. If someone did have the answer to her question, it was sure to be bad news.

Kaija Mae assumed right—nobody had an answer—if, in fact, anyone had even heard the question. But just as she began her songs again, her Shailma broke through; he did have the answer. Again she was right because it was not something good. Now that Shekinah had brought her heart the answer, she sincerely wished she had never asked the question.

What May Come

17

Shekinah's voice came straightaway to Kaija Mae. There were no long pauses as so often was the case. No waiting or seeking or searching—not this time.

My dear Kaija Mae, Shekinah began, *the winds are unusual. They are not winds from the normal stirring. They are not blowing in from the east or coming up from the south. No; not at all.*

The atmosphere is greatly stirred because of the war which is about to break out in the firmament. These winds are not of the air; they are of things in that place of the unseen where devils and angels dwell. It is that place where the Shamar Shailmas roam freely and the Nakah Warriors hide.

Kaija Mae knew very little about such things. Even though she and some of the others had been in Trilleah for so many years, nothing of a war had ever been mentioned. At least, she had not heard of it … and she had heard of many things.

She had overheard countless conversations between King Shrailzhar and his army and she had watched from her secret hiding places as the king had his minions set up this trap or that snare. In fact, Kaija Mae having knowledge of such things beforehand was the only way the Travelers had been able to do all that they'd done and still survive; without the knowledge Kaija Mae had passed on, the Travelers would have followed many wrong paths and some, would surely have brought doom.

The Travelers did not always know about the traps because Kaija Mae and the others often decided not to tell them. Surely, if they would have known about each and every trap and ploy and trick and ambush that had been set out for them, the Travelers would not have returned to the Dark Land so many times.

Much of the success of any of the Travelers' journeys was due to all the spying, snooping, and tedious watching that Kaija Mae and the others had done while the rest were away. So much work was done between the days when the Solstice Gates opened themselves up to the Travelers that just thinking about it now gave Kaija Mae a headache.

Yes, Kaija Mae, Aviel, Tahlia, and the others who had been stuck in this fateful land from the beginning, had seen much. They had released most of the smaller traps before the Travelers could return and three times they had to remove incredibly large snares at the gates so that they would open. Kaija Mae and the others had risked their own souls many times for the sake of Jennifer and the Travelers.

Oh, the king's army could certainly put together a phenomenal trap; there was no doubt about that. But never in all her years stuck in this forlorn land had Kaija Mae heard talk about war. The old lady knew the Shailmas were aware of much more than any of the Travelers because they dwelt in the unseen realm of the atmosphere. There must be so much going on there and for just a second, Kaija Mae wished she could see into it that realm like the Shailmas did.

She knew that was not possible, at least she was fairly certain it wasn't, so she listened carefully to Shekinah now.

"For sure" she whispered to the air, "Shekinah must know everything about this war and all that goes on in the unseen realm."

Kaija Mae, Shekinah continued, *this is the war that will end all wars. It is the war that King Shrailzhar has been trying to avoid from the start of Trilleah. But he knew—from the very beginning he knew—it would come and now, this very day, it is upon him.*

She shook her head in confusion.

Why would the king build a land that he knew he wouldn't be able to keep? How did that make any sense? The poor girl pondered the things of the deep—those things much too deep for a mere mortal to understand—and for a time, Shekinah was quiet, letting her ponder.

He knew that when one of the mortals would consider such inconsiderable things, they would quickly come to the necessary conclusion that they knew very little. This realization—that they understood nothing—was where they needed to land before they would look up and rely on the ones who knew it all.

If mere mortals ever thought they might have an understanding of things of the deep, they may stop listening for their Shailmas. They very well might stop asking questions, and stop obeying things they knew nothing about. It was a wise Shailma who let their mortal ponder rather than always giving answers where no questions had been asked.

Finally, after seeing Kaija Mae come to the end of her own understanding, Shekinah came to her once more.

This war, my dear, is being fought for the Travelers' souls and the final ownership rights to the Kingdom of Trilleah. If King Shrailzhar can win this war—and he truly believes that he can—he will own the souls of the only warriors left in all the earth who have the boldness and the unshakeable belief in the Shailmas. Then, Trilleah will be his legal kingdom for eternity.

No other will be able to come against him again, for what is legal in the unseen realm holds much more power and authority than what is legal in the seen one.

None will be able to remove Trilleah or enter it or do any damage to it again. The Solstice Gates will be closed and locked tight for all eternity. The Trows will have all rights to roam the earth, and steal the souls of those who die. No more will heaven be able to receive those souls for they will rightfully and legally belong to Trilleah.

Shekinah could see that Kaija Mae was getting paralyzingly fearful for even though she did not admit it often—and certainly, never out loud—she knew the dreadful King Shrailzhar did have great and mighty power over many things.

She wanted to sing and calm herself, but when she opened her mouth no words would come. For the first time since arriving in Trilleah, Kaija Mae was without a song; the butterflies that had been swirling in her belly suddenly turned into bats, making her wretchedly sick. Before she could get herself twisted into a tizzy, Shekinah opened the girl's ears once again, and she heard more of his explanation; more understanding came to her still.

Do not fret, Kaija Mae. While you may know King Shrailzhar and much of what he is capable of, you do not know who leads the Shamar Shailmas for that One has never been seen. Even we Seraphic Shailmas do not know Him; we have never beheld His great beauty. We know OF Him because of the Shamars, and we see the outcome of some of His power, but because of those great powers that He alone holds, we cannot look upon Him lest we die.

Suddenly, Kaija Mae lifted up her head and great peace was upon her. The bats turned back into butterflies and the butterflies settled in her belly. It seemed that such information should cause Kaija Mae even more fear, but in truth, it was the opposite that she felt.

If this was true, what Shekinah was telling her about a Being so powerful that even the Shailmas could not look at Him in case they died, then what would that mean for herself and the others? What if they saw Him. Was there ever a time they might see Him? She shuddered from the bottom of her insulated feet to the top of her head at such an overwhelming thought—but not from fear!

So that One, then, Kaija Mae asked, *that One will be fighting?*

Oh no! No, no, no. The Nameless One is in charge—that One whom we cannot look upon. But He will not be fighting. King Shrailzhar will not be fighting either. He will be watching—they both will be. But neither the Nameless One nor King Shrailzhar will be fighting in this War of the Firmament, Shekinah continued.

It is their jobs to give the orders, to release power where it is required and authority to whom it is due. It is not their jobs to fight.

Kaija Mae was confused but much less afraid than before Shekinah had brought some understandings of the deep to her mind. If she had to choose, she'd rather be deeply confused than horribly afraid and so, while she remained unhappy with the situation, she was content to be confused.

The beautiful old woman, who remained stuck inside this teenager's body, opened her mouth to call out to Bella. She wanted to talk with her and see if she had known of such things that Kaija Mae had just become aware of. She didn't call Bella's name, though, for when she opened her mouth, a song was released instead.

Kaija Mae was fairly certain her songs had come from Shekinah all along but had never known for sure. Now, when she looked into her mind and saw him there, she knew they must. Her Shailma gave her a small nod and suddenly, she had no doubt about where her songs came from.

Normally when Kaija Mae sang, her songs were quiet and shy almost, like she didn't care for anyone to hear her, but not this time. This time she sang loudly … powerfully even. But no matter, the words went unheard because the winds had become deafening by now. The pounding air took her words and tossed them away, into the wind. She sang anyway, even if nobody could hear her. Her voice was powerful and moaning almost, and the words—even though she couldn't understand any of them—filled her full with confidence.

What Kaija Mae did not yet understand, was that a word spoken, whether heard or unheard, went into the atmosphere and stayed there. Every word ever spoken or sang, no matter how loud or quiet, would eventually rise into the firmament and become a weapon. Whether the words became a weapon in the hands of a Shamar Shailma or a weapon in the hands of a Nakah, depended completely on the words themselves. And so, it made no difference whether or not Kaija Mae's songs were heard by the Travelers. What did matter was that her songs were equipping the Shamar Warring Shailmas, which always was —of course—the very purpose of the songs.

The Travelers could barely stand upright anymore. It wasn't because the wind was getting strong—although that was happening—it was because they were exhausted. None of them had sat or rested or eaten for a very long time and their bodies ached from having to walk so cautiously hour after hour. They each knew that if they didn't find shelter soon, they'd have no need for any. The winds would just blow them over and the intense heat that was coming up from the ground would consume them as it had done to their food earlier, and as it was doing to the bushes now.

Quite suddenly, an enormous ball of fire was carried through the sky on the wings of the wind and landed right in the middle of the Travelers who were desperate for shelter. It didn't hit any of them directly, but it did manage to singe a bit of Pierce's hair as it hit the ground and spouted up close to him.

Large chunks of smoldering ash were thrown around as the fireball hit the ground hard. Some were tossed this way, some were thrown that way. But no matter which direction the pieces of ash were flung, every single place they landed burst into flames. Some were small and instantly extinguished by the strong winds. Others were not small and continued burning. Still others became quite large in a small amount of time, and the wind pushed the flames along fiercely.

The Travelers tried to step on the smaller flames, putting them out, but it made no difference. Each one they'd put out, two more would begin.

When one large ball of fire hit Sam in the pant leg, he jumped back, twisting his foot on an exposed tree root and he toppled over. Naturally, he thrust out his hands to catch himself, and Matt immediately lunged forward to grab him but couldn't get to him in time. Sam's left hand hit the dirt hard and was instantly burned to the bone. A yellowish liquid oozed out of the open flesh and ran down his arm as Matt yanked him back up.

Sam's hand touched the ground for only a second, but that was all it took. It looked dreadful, with the burned flesh hanging from it like a peeled banana. It looked like it had melted right off the bone. He screamed out in great anguish and for a desperately long time. The others could see the agony on his face, and they could tell he was screaming because, well, even when one can't hear the screams of another, they do tend to contort the face and make it noticeable.

Sam's face was telling a story amidst the thunderous roaring winds that the others easily read. That story had many words that all meant the same thing …

Pain … agony … wretchedness … suffering.

Tahlia was closest to Kaija Mae, so she moved her ear right beside Kaija Mae's ear and screamed as loudly as she could.

"We need shelter." Kaija Mae nodded and moved to where Bella and Pierce stood, staring at Sam in horror. She put her lips right between their ears and with all her voice, screamed the same thing that she'd just heard from Tahlia.

"WE NEED SHELTER!"

They both nodded. Even though they were all shaken from the fireball that had just landed in the midst of them and exploded into a thousand pieces, Pierce, Bella, Aviel, and Tahlia went to work looking for shelter. It did not have to be all that suitable really; anything was better than what they had now—which was nothing. There was not even an overhanging tree branch where they stood. There was nothing they could see that might be an acceptable shelter, no matter how hard they strained their eyes or cranked their necks.

Kaija Mae moved to where Matt was trying to console poor Sam, but there was nothing that would bring any amount of peace. She could see that Matt was trying to tell the boy who was in such terrible agony something—she watched his lips move but couldn't hear the words.

She heard nothing except the howling winds that had picked up even more and were now screaming and scurrying around each Traveler, wrapping them in horror and dread.

"Did you hear something?" Jennifer asked Judah. She was leaning on his shoulder, reasonably comfortable yet horribly wretched, watching the lightning and listening to the howling winds, but now she shot upright. "There it is again," she shrieked. She sat perfectly still with only the balls of her eyes moving back and forth and up and down as if searching with her eyeballs would make her ears hear more clearly.

"I don't hear ..."

"Shhhh," Jennifer hushed her brother. He too now sat upright from his uncomfortable place of leaning against the rocks. He didn't hear anything other than the wind that insisted on hurling all sorts of debris into their little shelter, so instead of trying harder, he watched his sister's face. She certainly thought she had heard something.

They sat for a long while this way; Jennifer being perfectly still and listening intently while moving only the balls of her eyes this way and that—Judah also sitting perfectly still and watching his sister. He was getting tired of this … and impatient and uncomfortable. He was about to lay back against the hard rocks when she yanked on his arm, jolting him upright.

He would have ripped his arm away and been angry because he was already perturbed and really, if you consider all things, anger and perturbedness are very close neighbors. It would not have taken much to move him out of his perturbed state and right into the neighborhood of anger, but he did not go there because after all, he heard loud and clear whatever it was that she has been going on about.

Clear as a rainbow on a sunny day, he heard it. It was most assuredly not the wind … and it was close.

"Judah," she shrieked. "There it is again!"

Dark Voices

18

"What is that?" Jennifer whispered. She finally moved her head and looked right into Judah's eyes. "Judah, what was that sound?" she demanded as if he would know.

He didn't, of course, and so he shrugged his shoulders but tuned his ears in even more painstakingly, just in case the sound came again. It did. And it was closer than before; much closer. There was no way to make out what it was, though, for it was something neither of the twins had heard before.

They huddled closer together and slouched down as far as they could slouch inside their little shelter. Suddenly, both Judah and Jennifer wished for their cloaks. They hoped the unusually large bushes outside would help hide them or hide the entire shelter maybe, but that quickly became doubtful as the hands lurking in the wind reached out and pulled a few of the bigger bushes out by the roots, as if they were nothing more than the smallest of weeds.

"I miss Bella," Jennifer wailed. "She'd know what to do!"

The poor girl was letting so much fear grip her heart that it was becoming more and more difficult to keep it under control.

"I know, Jelly Bean," her brother said. "I miss her too." While he tried on the outside to console his anguishing sister, Judah was very busy on the inside begging Shemaiah to help him help her.

He heard a few things, but was so confused that he didn't know whether to encourage his sister with thoughts of how their auntie was fine and well-hidden in a perfect shelter of her own somewhere near, or if he should suggest that Bella was likely having enough difficulties of her own to worry about the twins. Neither would have made Jennifer feel any better and chances were good that both suggestions would have upset her even more. Judah kept his mouth shut and said nothing at all.

The twins, of course, didn't realize that not too far away, their auntie Bella was in desperate need of help. Pierce had taken her by the hand and together they'd led the others into a shelter that, even though they were unaware of it, was already occupied.

They would soon find out, however, for the deeper Pierce and the others wandered inside, the more the smell of sulfur burned their noses. Their eyes began to water like crazy until they could barely see.

"Everybody, hold hands," Bella whispered. In this shelter, they were so far down inside of its belly that the winds could no longer be heard, so whispering was sufficient.

It was dark—black dark—so finding another's hand to hold was challenging. They did try, though, and eventually one by one, they each found the others. Even though they had found each other and were trying to hold on, it was not working. They needed one hand to cover their noses while the second was required to wipe the tears from their burning eyes.

Finally, fully frustrated, Bella made a different suggestion.

"Okay listen," she said softly. "Everyone grab the collar of the person in front of you. That way we all have one hand to wipe our faces with." That made more sense and is exactly what they did. Bella shoved Pierce in front of her and Matt was at the back holding onto the collar of Aviel with one hand and the shirt of Sam with the other.

Sam, the poor boy, had gone into shock. At least he wasn't feeling the pain of his hand at the moment, but neither was he steady on his feet because of it. The tall boy was dizzy and sick to his stomach, and his mind was in and out of a normal state of consciousness. All of this made it very difficult for Matt to keep up with the rest while making sure Sam stayed with them.

"There is it again," Jennifer whispered. "It sounds like it's right above us!" Judah stood up and pulled his sister to her feet as well.

"Here," he whispered and gently shoved her behind him. "Get behind me and stay behind me. No matter what, Jennifer, stay behind me, do you hear? Do you hear me, Jelly Bean?"

She did, but Jennifer had no intention of staying behind her brother. After all, she might be a girl, but that was no reason to hide behind her brother. She was strong and stubborn and brave—very brave—and she was, after all, a Princess Warrior. *Princesses might hide behind their brothers, but not warriors. Warriors never hide.*

I am not about to hide either, she told herself.

With her self-thoughts raging in her mind, it built great courage in her belly and she stepped out from behind her bossy—but concerned—brother.

"I will not!" she huffed. "I'm sorry, Judah, but I won't hide and let you face whatever is out there alone …"

"But Jennif … Ugh … Oh fine," Judah sighed. He knew when to argue with his sister and when to admit defeat. She was much tougher than she appeared and far too stubborn for him to convince her of something she refused to be convinced of and so, he gave up trying. "Just be careful, Jelly Bean, please?" he added.

"Well, of course, I'll be careful," she snapped. "I'm not a fool!" He knew she was no fool, but sometimes even the wisest ones can be foolish, and that was what he was afraid of.

"I know," he muttered.

All the while the twins were deciding who would hide and who would not, and which one was foolish and which one was brave, the noises continued. Louder and louder they echoed until finally, the twins had to cover their ears.

Their little hideout was just that—little.

Simeon, was there nowhere bigger than this for us to be? Jennifer asked her Shailma. She didn't expect an answer nor did she receive one. She pictured in her mind that any shelter the others had found by now was sure to be much, much larger than this one. This one was no bigger than a rat hole! That's exactly what Jennifer felt like too, hunching down inside this little jut hoping not to be found by anything that might be looking for them.

"It's a good thing they found their own shelter because this one sure wouldn't have fit us all." She grumped and whined and complained to herself all the while, deeply thankful that she and her brother were not in the middle of the wind or in front of whatever it was that was making such a ruckus just a few feet away.

A low rumbling growl could be heard now. Jennifer wanted to ask Judah if he heard it … or what it could be … or if he was afraid, but the sound was so near to the opening that she dared not open her mouth. Both the twins were trying to breathe through their noses, but the sulfur was so strong that they had no choice but to breathe through their mouths and fight choking on the thick air.

A cough was stirring in Judah's throat. The smoke and sulfur were coating the inside of his mouth and had moved down to the bottom of his throat, and now a cough was fighting to come out. As quietly as he could, Judah tried to rumble his throat softly. That only made it worse. He cleared his throat quietly, and Jennifer pulled hard on his hand that she had been squeezing between both of her own.

Judah looked at her with big eyes, and she knew he was in trouble. She didn't say a word, but with hand motions, suggested he lift the collar of his shirt over his mouth. He did, but it didn't help. It was too late.

A loud cough erupted from her brother. He tried to cover it, oh, how hard he tried, but it was of no use. Judah began a loud and out-of-control coughing fit that stirred up the dust and the air. Whatever had been growling just above them, suddenly fell silent.

Pierce, who had been in front of the others, suddenly stopped. It was dark, so even though Pierce stopped, nobody else did. Bella ran into the back of him and likewise and so forth and on and on until everyone had run into the back of everyone else.

"Did we come to the end?" Matt asked. He was sure hoping so because he needed a rest from helping Sam. Nobody replied.

"Is there a problem?" Kaija Mae wondered loudly. Again, nobody replied. Of course, Pierce had his hand up in the air to try and get everyone to hush, but nobody could see it, so nobody hushed.

"What's going on, Pierce?" Bella whispered. She had a feeling that something was indeed going on, so she used the quietest voice she had.

"Listen …" was all Pierce replied.

She listened.

They all listened.

Grrrrwwwllllll, is what they heard.

Grrrrrrrrrrrrwllllllllllllllll.

Nobody moved.

Even Sam was able to hold his moaning to a quiet lull. Matt could hear him and felt sick to his stomach over the anguishing pain the poor boy must be feeling.

There was unmistakably something growling in that cave—or whatever it was into which they had wandered. Pierce was angry and let his Shailma know it. Now, he was not one to talk to his Shailma often, so when he did, he probably should not have been rebuking him. One does not rebuke a Shailma, after all. It is the Shailmas who do the rebuking and the correcting and the leading and the scolding; not the other way around. No, it was never wise to rebuke a Shailma.

Pierce was a stubborn one, though, and right now with Sam behind him trying to stifle his painful moans, and something unseen in front of him growling lowly, Pierce didn't care. He carried right on fuming at his Shailma.

His Shailma cared, though, and became quiet. This left an open space in Pierce's mind for the voice of the darkness that was subtly trying to wiggle its way in, to speak loud and clear.

It was not the Shailma who brought you here—it was I.

"Who are you?" Pierce whispered. His skin tingled and began sweating. Fear tightly gripped him. He didn't recognize this voice, yet somehow it seemed familiar. He could feel it stirring and it felt like the blinds on the windows of his mind were slowly being pulled down.

It is I, the Dark One, who you allowed in to lead you, the voice mocked.

I invited no one in. What are you talking about? Pierce was panicking and had no idea he should not be speaking to this one who was speaking to him. All the while the growling of whatever was in front of the Travelers was getting louder. The ones behind Pierce were pushing closer together and he was feeling overwhelmed with many things. Fear, dread, failure, and deep panic squeezed him from both the inside and the outside.

But there was nothing he could do—nothing at all, so he shrieked in the solitude of his mind. He screamed and hollered for his Shailma to help him, save him, rescue him and the others.

HELP ME NOW! he wailed over and over and over again until finally, after many cries, he heard a different voice … a comforting one … the one he knew. He saw the blinds that had been pulled down in his mind open slightly, letting in a crack of light.

I did not lead you here, Pierce, into this place. It is not a place of shelter for you and the others, not at all, is what he heard.

Then why did I come in here? How did I happen to see such a perfect place? Surely it was not my own eyes that saw the opening since I was looking in the opposite direction when my mind said, 'Go to the North fifteen feet.' Was that me, then?

No, his Shailma answered him straightaway. *It was not you either, Pierce. It was the Dark One who you invited in earlier. It was that one who led you and the others here and now it is that one whom you must get rid of or he will lead you straight to your grave ... and the others right along with you.*

None of this makes sense! Pierce was still feeling all the fear and dread he felt before he heard his Shailma, but now confusion was added to the growing pile of unwanted feelings rumbling in his belly. He had no idea what to do or who to listen to. He froze in his mind.

As the growling in the cave was so close now that it sounded like it was right in front of his face, he came to himself and again begged his Shailma to help. His stomach emptied its contents into his mouth, and he wanted to spit it out. Oh, how he wanted to spit it out. But with whatever was making its presence known so close now, Pierce dared not and held it, gagging, inside of his mouth for as long as he could.

Sometimes when the way ahead seemed too hard, one could turn around and retrace their steps back. This was not one of those times, though. Neither the way ahead nor the path back was acceptable … or safe.

For Trilleah

19

King Shrailzhar gave some final instructions to the head of the Nakah Warriors. "You are not to touch the Travelers or do them any harm. Not even a hair on the heads of the mere mortals is to be touched … they belong to ME!" he wailed. "Destroy as many of the Shamar Shailmas as you can and bring me the tails of their beasts so I can know how many you have conquered."

He spit and frothed at the mouth as he spewed out his deplorable orders. When he finished, the king raised his sword high in the air and with a final shout, dug his spiked boots into the sides of the dragon on which he sat.

"FOR TRILLEAH!" he shrieked.

"FOR TRILLEAH!" The 45,000 Nakah Warriors echoed back. As soon as they did, the Dark Land shook and trembled terribly just for a moment, as though it had a quick and sudden shiver; then, it was eerily still. The sky turned a deep shade of red. The moon had refused to come out from behind its place of hiding on this night, and now, all of Trilleah knew why.

The fireballs that had been hurled to the ground suddenly stopped, but all the fires, no matter how small, burned on. They did not spread throughout the land, which was unexplainable because one would expect the atrocious winds to make any size of fire spread quickly. The lightning stopped immediately as though it too, went into hiding from what it must have known was sure to be the beginning of a terrible battle.

The sea, which the Travelers had seen earlier, became as still as glass. If one saw it now, they'd wonder if it was a sea at all for there was not even one wave or wrinkle, billow, or ripple to be found.

Suddenly, and without warning, even the winds stopped. They no longer swirled or twisted or blew. Not even a whistle or a whisper could be heard in the land. It was completely silent—as if the entirety of Trilleah wanted to hide from the unstoppable war that had now been set into motion.

Erebus, Cethin, Efah, and Kamenwati, who were the four Generals of the Nakah Warriors, raised their swords high in the air. The very second they brought their swords down, the 45,000 Nakah Warriors took off, racing into the firmament in search of the Shamar Shailmas. Every one of those dark shadowy warriors was filled with confidence that they would quickly overtake the Shamar Shailmas, making way for the Army of Shrailzhar to capture those beastly Curse Breakers.

The Shamars were quick—that fact was certainly not overlooked—and while the Nakahs may not have been as fast in flight, they were more shrewd and calculated in their war tactics. There was no level they would not stoop to, nothing to stop them from overcoming their enemy. At least, that's what they believed.

Now it must be said that the Shamar Shailmas were not hiding or trembling or just waiting to be attacked. Oh no, not at all! They were ready and strategically stationed all throughout the firmament, waiting for their moment to be released and overtake the Nakahs. No fear would be found in them. There were 39,277 Shamar Shailmas in total who'd been called for battle and were ready for the War of the Firmament, although there were many, many more who had been previously assigned to other tasks.

Erebus took 11,250 Nakah Warriors to the east. Cethin took 11,250 Nakah Warriors to the south. Efah took 11,250 Nakah Warriors to the north, and Kamenwati took the remaining 11,250 Nakah Warriors to the west. They were all in search of the scheming Shamar Shailmas and would stop at nothing to find where they were hiding and overtake them.

The final orders that had been given by King Shrailzhar were this; to head into every corner of the land and once there, to encircle the skies. So, once the king's Generals led their allotted amount of Nakah Warriors to their corners of Trilleah, they spread out. The left side of one Nakah Warrior was firmly pressed against the right side of the next.

On and on they positioned themselves until those dreadful Nakah Warriors had stretched themselves clear from one side of the firmament to the other. They left no open spaces or holes in the atmosphere for the Shamars to slip through. They had successfully encircled the entire land, just as the king had commanded. Surely King Shrailzhar would be pleased.

Now in perfect position, Erebus, Cethin, Efah, and Kamenwati raised their swords. When the ones next to them saw, they raised their own swords, and so on and so forth, until all 45,000 Nakahs had their swords raised high. They sat exactly that way, in that same position, waiting for the Generals to swipe their swords across the heavens and bring them in front of themselves, sending the Nakahs forward.

The Nakah Generals believed that when their swords were pointing to the center, one from each direction, that wherever the points of the four swords crossed was where the enemy would be found. If the enemy were not there, the points of the swords would quickly lure them in like a supernatural magnetic force.

They believed that by symbolically slicing the heavens into four quarters, that one-quarter of the enemy's army—no matter who that enemy might be—would be rendered useless. Furthermore, one-quarter of the enemy's army would fall dead, another quarter of the enemy's army would become overwhelmed with confusion, which would leave only one-quarter of the enemy's army left to fight.

Of course, the Nakahs were dull-minded creatures and even though they were beings of the unseen world, they had never really been in a battle of such magnitude before. Until now, they never had a chance to test any of their theories, and so they would quickly find out that their theories were dreadfully wrong.

Because they had so many more warriors in their army than the Shamars had in theirs, it seemed that just by the very rule of common sense, the Nakah Warriors had a large advantage right from the beginning.

Jennifer and Judah stood paralyzed with fear. There was no way to tell if Judah's coughing fit had scared off whatever had been growling just a few steps away from where they hovered, or if it had gone quiet, waiting for the twins to emerge from their place of hiding.

They both wanted to ask the other what they thought, but of course, neither wanted to make the noise it would take to do so. Instead, they started making signals with their hands. Any conversation was tricky this way—or at least it would have been for anyone else. But because they were twins and often thought the same way, Jennifer and Judah realized how very easy communicating this way actually was.

They looked around for another way out of this rat hole, not that they had anywhere else to go. Jennifer began feeling her way along the walls and Judah looked up to the ceiling. The twins made a great effort to stay away from the floor, although it seemed less angry now.

Judah let some saliva drop from his mouth and land on the floor. Both the twins watched and expected it to sizzle as it had before. It didn't. It just sat there in a disgusting puddle. Judah wiped his shoe over it and spat again. Nothing. It seemed even the Sea of Acheron, which laid just beneath the thin layer of ground, had calmed itself considerably.

Neither Judah nor Jennifer found anything notable now to cause dreadful fear. So, with the greatest measure of caution, Judah crouched as low as he could to the ground without actually touching it. They were not secure enough in the temperature of the ground to let their flesh touch it just yet. He peered out of their shelter; only a quick glimpse at first, and then a full-on stare.

"Jennifer!" He sprang up and shouted to his sister, startling her. She jumped and banged her head.

"Ouch … Judah!" she wailed and slapped her brother on the shoulder. "What are you doing?"

"Jennifer, come look." He moved over a little to make room for his sister to stick her head out of the shelter. She was a little hesitant because of all they had run into the shelter to escape from, and she wasn't excited about going back into the middle of it. Finally, Judah persuaded her to look.

"Just look, please," he begged.

"Fine!" she huffed through gritted teeth.

Jennifer peeked quickly and pulled her head back in. She looked at Judah and peeked again, longer this time and with eyes stretched wide. Again she pulled her head back into the shelter and then it was her turn to startle Judah. She jumped up and down, clapped her hands, and squealed. She would have danced as well since she did love to dance, but there was no room for such silliness inside their cramped little shelter.

"What happened?" she squealed. "Judah, everything is still!"

"I know!" he answered with excitement wrapped around his words. "Did you see the sky? Did you see it?" Oh, Judah was far more excited about the stillness of the land then she remembered him being about anything before; at least anything in Trilleah.

She stuck her head out again and looked at the sky. "Oh, Judah," she sighed. "It's beautiful!" And indeed it was.

Whatever had been growling at the twins, was gone. In fact, the twins realized that everything was gone. There was not even a bug floating in the air. There were a few fires still burning, but they were mostly small now without the winds to keep them raging. The ground had cooled to an acceptable temperature, and the lightning had stopped striking.

In fact, except for the lack of color in Trilleah, it was almost an acceptable land. There was nothing frightening that they could see anywhere, and the sky—oh, it was a beautiful deep red. They assumed it was from the sunset, even though it had been a long while ago.

Jennifer looked for the moon, but couldn't find it. She didn't think it was odd, but she should have.

"Judah," she whispered. "Is the War of the Firmament over, do you think?"

"It must be," her brother naively replied.

You see, the twins had a grave error in their thinking. They thought what they had seen earlier, just before they found the cramped little shelter, was the war. They figured the horrendous winds, the bolting lightning, the boiling beneath the crust of ground and the balls of fire that had been hurling through the air were, in fact, the war.

Jennifer and Judah began to dance and jump and scream and shout and sing because they were sure that the war had been waged, and the Shamar Shailmas had won. They were overly confident that the stillness in Trilleah was because the War of the Firmament was over and the sky had opened itself to beautiful colors, and more colors would surely be painted across the rest of Trilleah soon.

They would be extraordinarily surprised, terribly horrified, outrageously appalled, when they found that the stillness of Trilleah and the color in the sky was because the war was just about to begin.

This moment, the one they thought signaled the end, was really the moment to signal the beginning.

It was absolutely, positively, hands down, without a doubt, the calm before the storm.

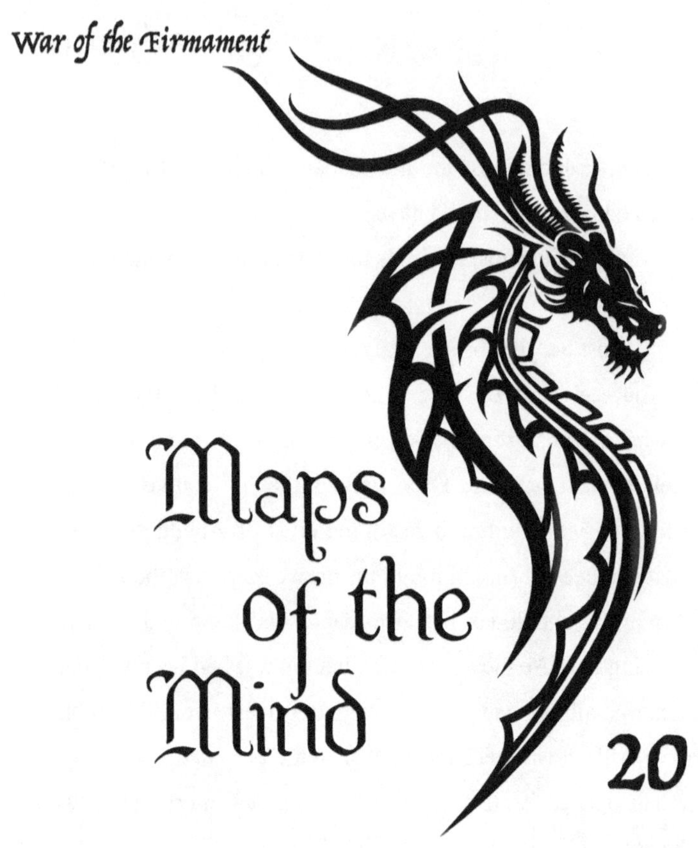

Maps of the Mind

20

"We have to find Bella," Jennifer squealed. She was very excited and had no doubt that in this land, even in peculiar places they'd never been and without any maps to lead them, she and her brother would find the others. "This is our chance, Judah!"

Jennifer was running ahead, already halfway down a skinny path which they were unable to see earlier because of the outrageous winds and the smoke and sulfur that had been shooting from the cracks in the ground. It seems the path had been there all along, only hidden by the storms of Trilleah.

Judah didn't waste any time arguing with her—she wouldn't have listened to him if he did—and within just a few seconds he was right behind her hurrying to catch up.

"Jennifer, wait …"

She was not about to wait. Jennifer had already waited too long to go and find Bella, Matt, and the others. That was all she'd been thinking about in that rat hole of a shelter. She was not going to wait any longer.

As they hurried, going back and forth between running for as long as they could and then walking just long enough to catch their breath, Judah finally hollered.

"Jennifer, STOP! We don't know where we're going."

Sometimes when his sister got excited about something, she'd just go. With all her might she'd go. It might be completely the wrong direction, however, and while sometimes back home in Westlock that was okay, here in Trilleah it was not okay.

If they went the wrong direction here, especially running, when they had no idea how much time they had or if it was the right way or who they might come upon or even if the ground might still be bubbling somewhere along the way, it was a bad idea; a very bad idea. Judah was going to have to get his sister to slow a little and figure this thing out—if such things were possible.

Jennifer stopped instantly. She bent over to catch her breath and realized her brother was probably right. There was only one thing to do and she did it. As she was hunched over, her head in her hands and her elbows on her knees, she searched for the one and only being who could help.

"Simeon," she whispered. "Help."

Now sometimes, when one of the Travelers was desperate for help, they used many words to ask for it. First, they'd take the time to explain the problem as they saw it (as if the Shailmas didn't already fully know such things). Then, they'd suggest all sorts of ways that their Shailma might help to fix the problem. They'd often offer some possible solutions, and almost always, the Travelers would spend so long talking that it took a long time to get an answer.

But not today; not this time. Jennifer had learned somewhere along the way that Simeon already knew all problems before she did, and he already had the solutions. She didn't need to remind him of anything or coax him into helping her. Helping her was the very reason he existed, so it seemed.

So, that was the only word she whispered now.

"Help," she muttered again under her breath. No sooner had she uttered the one-word simple request, then a picture popped into her mind; more of a map of sorts. It was like someone had turned on a television set in her mind and that's the channel on which it was pre-set.

Now, it was not a map like the Living Maps. Nothing sprang to life; no mountains rose up and no valleys dug themselves deep. There were no winds or armies or anything notable whatsoever. It was just a map, plain and simple, with a faint, narrow path etched out. That was all she needed.

She lurched upright. "Judah," she squealed. "I know where they are!"

"What? How?" he asked. He was bewildered to be sure, but nothing surprised him with Jennifer anymore. If she could get pulled into an adder's pit, find the tablet, and get back out of the adder's pit, surely knowing where to find Bella and the others shouldn't be a surprise to him. He knew Jennifer had seen things the rest of them hadn't.

"Simeon showed me," she replied. Oh, she was laughing now, so hard that she had to bend over again and hold her belly. It was one of those laughs that come from somewhere so far down inside that you didn't even know your belly went that far. It was one of those laughs where the more you laugh, the more it hurts, but the more it hurts, the more you laugh. Nonetheless, that was the laugh coming from his sister and Jennifer couldn't stop it now. It had taken her. Soon, as that kind of laugh often does, it caught ahold of Judah as well and the two of them were doubled over laughing and wheezing and gasping for breath.

If they would have known the Army of Shrailzhar was watching the twins carefully and the king of Trilleah himself had his eye on them, they wouldn't have been laughing. They would have been screaming and running to find a place to hide—anywhere! Even the rat hole of a shelter they'd just popped out of would have sufficed.

But they didn't know and so they carried on, laughing and crying and moaning and groaning because the laughing hurt their bellies so much that it made them laugh all the more.

"This way," Jennifer squealed and tried to catch her breath and get control of the laughing. The land remained quiet and the twins were full of joy, for they were enjoying the stillness and the idea that the war was over, and that they would be finding the last tablet in peace. The twins were comfortable in believing they had won and all that was left were a few loose ends to tie up.

Meanwhile, all the time the twins were laughing, Bella was hovering behind Pierce in the quiet darkness of the belly of the cave. They could not see that the land had calmed itself and was now breathless, so they assumed it wasn't. They assumed everything outside of this cave was the same as when they'd stumbled into it.

All they could hear down here in the damp underbelly of wherever they had wandered, was the weeping and anguish of Sam, the hushed voice of Matt trying to calm him, and the snarly breaths of whatever was still in front of them.

Pierce didn't have any idea what to do. He realized in an instant, like a lightbulb coming on in his mind, that it was not his Shailma who'd led him here, although he still didn't understand how he had allowed a dark voice to take up space in his mind. He was thoroughly confused, to say the least.

It's the jealousy, he heard his Shailma whisper. *And your hateful anger toward Miriam.*

What? He knew he'd heard the thoughts since they were perfectly clear. But he did not know from whom they came. If he had unknowingly let a darkness into his mind, then how was he to know which voice he heard now?

Even as he thought such thoughts, the voice came again. *Pierce,* it said, *you know my voice. My voice brings calm and peace, the other does not. The other voice, the one unfamiliar to you, stirs up terrible things. The dark voice tells you that you have every right to be angry and encourages you to stay that way. The dark voice convinces you that being so very jealous of Jennifer is the right thing. The dark voice will never bring you any amount of peace. That's how you know.*

You know my voice, Pierce. Listen to it, or you will meet sure destruction.

Tell me this, the boy now pleaded desperately. *How do we get out of the belly of this pit? I thought I was leading them the right way, really I did. But now I know I led them right into a trap of some sort. How do I get them out?*

If not for me, help me for them. It isn't their fault I let a darkness inside. At least, let them go! Whatever I must pay to save them, let me pay it! He was ranting silliness but meant every word with all his heart.

That was all that was required, and without even knowing it, Pierce's words put up barriers in his mind that forced the dark voice into silence. His own Shailma came to him again, clearer than ever before.

That's a brave request, Pierce. And so, I shall grant it. I will help you because your concern is now for the others, and not for yourself. Up until this very moment, you cared about yourself more than any others. But you have shown that you care about these others also, and so, I shall help you. You have acknowledged your errors and are willing to pay for those errors.

You still have to silence the dark voice and take back all access you've allowed it, but this is not the place. First, let's get you out of this dungeon and then we will deal with the dark voice.

That sounded like a fine idea to Pierce. He'd happily do whatever was required to silence the dark voice AFTER they were out of this deep snare. The thoughts of what waited for them outside were not great, not for Pierce or any of the others who were trapped in this pit. They each assumed that whatever dark things were going on outside before they fell into this dungeon would continue to go on if they ever got out of it.

A few turns this way, a twist or two that way, and straight on ahead, and Judah and Jennifer found themselves nowhere that looked familiar. Of course, Trilleah was incredibly large, and they had not traveled very much of it at all—not really—so being in unfamiliar territory wasn't surprising. Jennifer insisted this was the way the map in her head had shown.

"Look over there," she whispered to her brother.

He looked. "I don't see anything," Judah said.

"Further up, just above that hill," she whispered again.

"Why are you whispering all of a sudden?" he asked. He was getting frustrated and wondered who might be more confused—him or his sister. He decided to try and see what she was pointing at before making the decision … as though it was his to make.

He looked where Jennifer was pointing. There was a sign or something etched into the rocks just above a small opening.

"What is that?" he asked. Jennifer shrugged, but whatever it was, her belly began hurting for a whole different reason … reasons she didn't know or like. She wished the laughing would return, but knew it wouldn't.

"Do you think they're inside?" she asked. Now it was Judah's turn to shrug. He had a feeling that they were and it made sense. This was the only place he and Jennifer had seen where anyone could hide out. Nevertheless, there was something eerie about it; something that made them want to stay on this side of the small opening.

"I dunno, Jennifer," he whispered. "There's something I don't like here, but I don't know what it is. The air feels different; cold." She knew what he meant because she felt the same.

"But Simeon wouldn't have led us here for no reason," she argued in not much more than a whisper. Suddenly, any confidence she'd felt a few moments earlier couldn't be found now.

The twins were looking this way and that, all around, as if something might give them a clue as to what was making this place so uncomfortable for them. Nothing stood out that they could see. But then again …

"What's that?" Jennifer asked. She bent down and spit on the ground to check the temperature of it. Nothing happened. She did it again. Nothing happened the second time either, so she carefully touched her fingers to the ground right where there seemed to be a recent puddle of something red and sticky that had tried escaping through the ground. It should have seeped into the dirt, but it hadn't.

"Here," she held her fingers up to her brother. "What is this?" She already knew the answer but was too afraid to say it out loud.

"Looks like blood."

He was right, of course, for that's precisely what it was.

Jennifer jumped up and squealed as quietly as she could, wiping her fingers on her pants, trying to get every shred of the red liquid off. Her eyes grew large as she slowly turned to look at her brother. His eyes had also grown large as he looked at her, then back to the ground where the puddle of blood lay.

"Look! There!" he said and pointed to another few drops of the same red liquid.

"And there," Jennifer whispered. There seemed to be a lot of what they decided was the blood of one of the Travelers. The twins, each in their own mind, for it wasn't anything either wanted to speak out loud, wondered if it was the blood of one of their friends, or … of all of them.

Now the path veered off into two different directions. Judah and Jennifer could follow the path one way, which would lead them away from the opening in the rock, or they could follow it the other way, which would lead them straight into the very opening that was making them shudder. There was no doubt which way the other Travelers had gone.

"Judah," she said, and without whispering any more words, Judah knew which words were on his sister's lips.

The twins looked at each other and then back to the blood. Back and forth they went, saying no words but forcing their eyes back and forth between the other's face … and the blood … and the small opening in the cave.

Finally, they each looked directly into the eyes of the other and at the same time they whispered, "they're inside."

Ghastly Howls

21

A blast of horror spread across Judah's face and he glanced back to his sister, expecting to see the same look mirrored in hers. He didn't. What he did see was glee. Complete excitement had poured into his sister's face, filling it with color. Her cheeks were suddenly rosy, and her eyes sparkled.

"Is that a good thing, Jenny?" he asked. Judah was confused now. His fragile sister seemed to be ignoring the pools of blood around them and the fact—well, it wasn't a fact yet, but they were pretty sure it would be—that their friends and their auntie were inside that cave. Judah could come up with no good reason whatsoever for Jennifer's odd reaction to such a dreadful assumption.

There was no doubt that at least one of their friends was badly injured. All sorts of grotesque pictures and horrible thoughts ran through Judah's head, from bad to terrible to altogether hideous and unthinkable. After all, that was a lot of blood. It seemed to trail off, as far as they could tell, in the direction away from the cave, and there was a lot here, in front of the cave. Even worse, it went right INTO the cave.

"Judah," Jennifer squealed in delight. "We found them!"

It didn't seem to be bothering her that they would have to venture into an unknown dark cave to retrieve the others, or that whatever had caused the blood on the outside of the cave may be hiding inside of the cave. Jennifer never considered the possibility that only one of the Travelers may be inside of this cave and that whoever that one was, was the one who was bleeding. It never dawned on her, seemingly, that what they might find inside the cave may be … well …

No thoughts about whoever was the one bleeding may have been dragged into the dark hole in front of them, and now she was suggesting they just march right on inside to find whoever—or whatever—was in there. Judah was very displeased with her obvious lack of thought on the matter.

Nonetheless, Judah took a deep breath and followed his fearless—or foolish—sister, right into the mouth of what could soon become their graves. Judah crossed his fingers and prayed and hoped and hoped and prayed that whatever had dragged one of his dear friends into the dark passageway was long gone.

He wouldn't have gone in at all, but Jennifer had already made up her mind, and when his sister made up her mind about something, that was the way it was going to be. No amount of common sense or rationalization would stop her. She had far too much faith in that Shailma of hers, and if he had led her to this place, then nothing would keep her out of it.

Deep inside the shadowless cave where the twins had now headed, the others remained frozen in fear and drowning in despair. They were utterly stuck between whatever was growling and snarling in front of Pierce, and Sam, who had finally passed out from unbearable pain. The lanky boy was being held up by Matt and Aviel … and he was heavy.

The Travelers couldn't go forward and they didn't know the way back. At least the ravaging sounds of Sam's pain had been quieted, but the ones at the front of the line, Bella and Kaija Mae mostly, were very worried. They knew the dreadful moans and whimpers of pain had stopped, but they didn't know why. Nobody dared to ask, just in case this beast—or whatever was in front of them—was set off.

So far, whatever was hovering in front of them, sniffing the air and pawing in the dirt, seemed content to do just that. But they had no way of knowing how long that contentment would last. They went from holding their breath to letting it out slowly and filling their lungs up again, all done safely under the dirt-smeared collars of their shirts.

The sulfur smell was a little less putrid right at the moment, which was a slight relief to the Travelers huddled in the dark, but the smell coming from Sam's burned flesh took its place. What was even more disturbing, was hearing that something was definitely moving in behind them. They heard footsteps and chatter.

Matt whispered to whoever was in front of him, wondering if someone else had heard it, or maybe it was his imagination. They heard it too and began whispering about it. As quietly as they could whisper and still be heard, which was very quiet indeed, was exactly how loud they dared to whisper.

Each noise echoed inside this hollow cave, making everything seem much worse. The snorts and sniffs and pawing of whatever was in front of them reverberated throughout the cave, hitting one wall and bouncing off another. The footsteps of whatever was coming up behind them did the same. The closer the footsteps came, the louder the echoes were until finally, the echoes of the footsteps mingled with the echoes of the beast and in one moment, all that could be heard were echoes.

Whoever was coming from behind must have heard the echoes of the beast and halted. The beast surely heard the sounds of something in the cave and became quiet. Whatever the reasons, the cave quite suddenly became eerily silent both from the front ... and from the back.

It was dark where they stood and so, of course, nobody could see anything whatsoever. If there was even a spark of light, they'd have noticed that the eyeballs of every Traveler had grown large. They had all opened their eyes wide, trying desperately to get a glimpse of what was in front of them—or what had come up behind. If they could only get a shadow or a glimpse of another Traveler, it might have helped bring some amount of confidence, but there was not a shred of light available to find either.

Nobody wanted to move or think or breathe. Each cried out desperately in silence to their Shailmas. Mishan came to Matt and instructed him to hold out his hand and whisper his own name, identifying himself. This took a great amount of courage and even though Matt was excellent at acting like he was courageous, the truth was that he wasn't courageous at all.

He didn't do as Mishan had asked, at least, not immediately. So, it was a good thing that Shemaiah spoke a similar thing to Judah. Judah listened right away, for his fear was much less than Matt's at the moment. Judah didn't realize the Travelers were in front of him, due to their perfect silence and the blinding darkness, nor did he realize that they'd been trapped for a very long time by whatever creature was blocking them.

If Judah had known such things, he'd surely have turned around and headed straight back out. It's a good thing, sometimes, when one does not have all the information for a particularly difficult situation. Often, too much information halts what should never be halted. This was one of those times.

And so, Judah gingerly put his hands out like a blind man feeling for a light switch. Softly, and barely more than a breath, he uttered his own name. He didn't whisper it and to say that he did would be a great exaggeration.

It wasn't heard; not at all. But Mishan grabbed ahold of it and carried it to Matt's ears. He would never have heard Judah if Mishan didn't deliver the sound to him. Matt was fearfully excited. He didn't know how to let Judah know they were in a very dangerous predicament without using words and without being able to see him.

Suddenly, he had an idea. Matt wiggled an arm free from under Sam, which made it hard to hold him up since Sam was a very tall boy. He hoped Aviel would feel the extra weight and take it upon himself. Otherwise, Sam would slump to the ground and again feel the incredible heat from down below—the very same heat that had wounded him so badly in the first place. They had to keep poor Sam upright; there was no doubt about that.

As Matt felt Aviel take much of Sam's weight, he reached out, wanting to find Judah's face, not his hands. He thought if he could find Judah's face, he could put his finger to his lips as some sort of sign language that would scream, "hush."

Soon, they did find one another, but not as they'd hoped.

As Matt had one hand held out and Judah still had his hands both out in front of him, it came as quite a surprise when a big shove came from behind Matt. Instead of gently finding the boy's face and trying to signal somehow to him to keep quiet, Matt ended up lunging forward and falling right on top of the twins.

"Oaf," came the sound from Jennifer as the wind was knocked from her.

Before Matt could notice that the ground had not burned their skin nor caused their clothes to go up in flames, he was scrambling to get back up to his feet. He so much expected the ground to be ablaze that he didn't realize at first that it wasn't.

"Judah," he whispered, for there was no need to be hushed in this particular moment since everyone was scrambling and mumbling and squealing. Matt tried to spill out as much information as possible before silence came and blanketed the Travelers again.

He found Judah's face and put his hands on the boy's cheeks just to be sure, even in the darkness, that Judah was listening carefully.

"Judah," he said, "is that you?"

"Who else would it be?" Judah chuckled. He still had no idea of what dangers lie just ahead of Pierce, nor what tragedy had fallen upon Sam.

"Listen carefully," Matt said sharply. He didn't understand Judah's lightheartedness, especially since Matt had clearly remembered what was going on outside of the cave. There was certainly nothing to be lighthearted about, and so he was confused.

"We're not alone in this dungeon. There's something up ahead and we've been trapped here, by whatever it is, for a long time. Pierce is at the front and is not giving any information at all. I don't think he can." And then, Matt had a strange thought. He didn't know where it came from but shared it with Judah nevertheless. "Pierce *was* at the front, and I *assume* he still is, but maybe something's happened to him. I don't know. I don't know anything ..."

Matt rambled as much information as he possibly could about their situation, and he knew Judah was listening. Likely, Jennifer was listening as well because he knew she was very close to where Judah had stood himself up. The only reason Matt knew she was there was because of the sound she'd made when the air was knocked out of her.

Quite suddenly, and before he could speak of what had happened to Sam, Matt stopped talking. After about ten seconds, he whispered to the others what the realization was that had fallen into his head. He presumed nobody else noticed what he was just realizing.

"I fell to the ground and didn't burn up!"

He had been so busy carrying Sam, and so focused on giving Judah information about what was ahead, that it didn't dawn on him that the ground had not consumed them all. Now that he realized it, he was again very confused.

The boy had no time to wonder about it because Jennifer spoke up. "We saw all the blood outside; that's how we found you!" She waited for someone to reply and didn't think she would have to ask what had happened or who was bleeding, but after a time of nobody offering any such information, she did ask.

"Is the blood from one of you?" she asked in her normal voice. Instead of an answer, she heard one, two, three, four voices hushing her. Jennifer slapped her hands over her mouth and raised her eyebrows. She hadn't realized she'd spoken so loudly, but with the instant reactions of the others, she knew she must have.

The beast that had been quieted in front of Pierce was disturbed now and began his low rolling growl again. Pierce froze, having to concentrate just to keep breathing. He pushed back slightly, frantically trying to move everyone backward. There was no other hope than to quietly sneak backward from the same way they'd come in.

Of course, even though they could not see in the dark, there was no way they could know if the creature could. Chances were pretty good that it could, they suspected.

Suddenly, the beast released a pain-riddled howl and slime and sludge was spewed across Pierce's face. He gagged and held his breath. Oh, the smell was completely dreadful. Everything within him wanted to turn around and run as fast as he could. He'd already decided that was a terrible idea since he'd spent a good deal of time pondering it earlier.

If even one person did not run fast enough, or fell and caused the others to trip, Pierce would be the one at the back—right in front of the beast. He'd be the one to become this unseen creature's lunch.

A group of people running frantically in the dark, when one of those people is unconscious, down a path they didn't know and couldn't navigate, was the stupidest idea of any possible stupid ideas. But right now, as Pierce was cringing and gagging with sludge dripping down his face, it seemed like it might not be that bad of an idea after all.

Whatever had caused that beast to howl, none of them knew. However, it also caused him to retreat a little and in just a minute or two, they heard whatever that thing was they'd not yet seen, whimper and drag itself back into the darkness.

It wasn't gone, certainly not, because they could still hear it. The growls had turned into whimpers and the pawing at the ground was replaced with the sound of the beast licking itself. Sometimes, even in the dark, things can be seen clearly by other senses, and this was seen very clearly. The beast had been stung or injured somehow and had retreated to a corner to whimper and lick its wounds.

Most of the Travelers were relieved and the cave echoed with one big sigh of relief. Not all of the Travelers were so easily delighted, however, and there were thoughts other than relief that lingered in Kaija Mae's mind as well as Bella's. If the beast that had been so threatening to them for so long had suddenly been wounded, then the question must be asked, what—or who—caused the injuries?

Even if that one beast had pulled back from the Travelers, there was no way to be sure there were not more just like him right around the very next bend or even worse … whatever had injured this beast may end up being a worse threat to the Travelers than the original one had been.

A King Enraged

22

One lonely flash of lightning streaked across the sky. That was it; just one. Nobody was out in the land to see it so it may not have mattered except …

The lightning was supposed to stay under the covers of the atmosphere. The entire sky was supposed to be hiding all activity as well as its darkness, which was why it had turned red. Well, the sky itself was not red, it was merely a reflection of what was simmering just beneath the floor of Trilleah. Nonetheless, the sky had been instructed to hide the darkness that usually covered it.

The king, however, did notice that one misplaced flash of lightning and became outraged that the land was disobeying his commands. After all, he had been the one to put the land together, and he would be the one to destroy it if ever it needed to be destroyed.

At this moment, King Shrailzhar was full of hope that the Nakah Warriors would defeat those pathetic Shamar Shailmas and he would soon be able to set up his eternal kingdom right here. He had it perfectly planned. Consequently, when he noticed the one faulty bolt of lightning shoot across the sky—his sky—he became enraged at such rebellious and willful disobedience.

King Shrailzhar immediately directed his sword to the sky and roared. The land released a small tremor, barely even noticeable, but it had to work very hard to keep itself from shaking apart. It had been commanded to be still, so any slight tremor caused great concern.

Trilleah knew the king was already angry at the lightning and did not wish to anger him further. There were no limits to where the brutish king of Trilleah would go to prove he was the one in charge.

The unspoken truth was that nobody really cared. If only that miserable wretch of a king would have let the souls of the Waiting Ones free, he could have his stupid land. Nobody would ever have bothered him again. Unfortunately, there was one very big problem with that.

If King Shrailzhar did not have all those souls he'd spent so long waiting for the Trows to steal, if he had not cursed them to remain in his land, then he would have nothing in his kingdom. A king cannot have a kingdom all by himself. He needs someone to be the king of. If he didn't have the souls locked away in Malleana Forest, he'd have no need for an army … and every good king needs an army, after all.

Yes, that most miserable King Shrailzhar would never let the souls of the Waiting Ones go free. In fact, he would never be satisfied with the ones he already had. He was a selfish and greedy king and always needed more and more souls in order to be satisfied.

More than once, the king's closest allies would try to persuade him to be satisfied with the number of souls that he'd cursed to Malleana Forest and more than once, he thought they might be right. He'd sometimes agree that he would be satisfied, but then, only a short amount of time would pass without gathering new souls before the king would get anxious and unsatisfied. His desire for more was altogether insatiable.

Each time, he grew more dissatisfied than he was the last time, so he'd send out as many Trows as he could spare and demand they each bring back a soul. Those who failed in their mission, those poor Trows who dared to return without a soul for the king to add to his ever-growing collection, would be put to a horrible death.

The king made sure that when he'd bring death to one of the Trows, the others would all see it. Every time that awful king would make an example out of the Trow and each time, he'd make the display of their torment just that much worse, all to persuade the others not to cross him.

Yes, Shrailzhar was a dreadfully selfish and greedy king indeed.

So now, of course, as he saw that the lightning had disobeyed his command from earlier today, he was outraged. As he thrust his sword toward the sky and bellowed, "Cursed be the lightning," the sky lit up like a fireworks display and a large number of lightning bolts that had been hiding behind the red reflection fell to the ground; one-third in all.

The moment those hit the ground, they shook and trembled. Within minutes, each one of them lost its glowing brilliance. They went black and crumbled into nothing more than piles of ash and soot. Just then, a light wind came by, swooping the piles up and carrying them away.

Oh, how dreadful the king was to discipline so much of the lightning for the actions of only one. But that was just the way he was, for truly, he was a despicable king.

Even the darkness wanted to hide from him, but of course, darkness is what hides everything else. The only thing that can hide darkness is light, and even then one might suppose that the darkness is not hidden at all, but merely exposed.

The sky had cracked open a small slit where the lightning had fallen through, and it remained that way. Other bits of sky that had shaken and been broken through earlier now stretched and pulled themselves back together just enough to cover the holes. But by doing so, the sky made itself much thinner than it should have been, and weak … too weak for what was to come.

Still standing with their swords pointing inwards all around the circle of that thin red sky, stood the Nakah Warriors. The final call had not yet been given, and so they waited. Even though the Nakahs were ready for battle, they had to give time for their trap to entice the Shamar Shailmas; that had not happened … yet … and so they waited.

The very second it did, a loud cry would go up from the four generals who sat ready in the four corners of Trilleah, and the army would move swiftly. That was their plan. However, they'd never actually come up against such an enormous battle, and so the Nakahs would not know for certain if their plan would work until they tried it.

They would find out soon enough.

The Shamar Shailmas had no need to hide the Travelers at the moment because the cave was doing that quite well. There were a few of the largest Shamars, however, stationed outside the entrance to that cave. The Travelers didn't know it, but there were also three Shamars who had gone into the cave with them.

Even though the battle had not yet begun, it was setting itself up, and the Armies of Shrailzhar had not forgotten their mission. They didn't need to wait, necessarily, for the Nakah Warriors to overpower the Shamar Shailmas. The very instant the Travelers were unattended and left exposed, the army was to go and retrieve the twins and take the souls of the rest. That was their job—to get the twins.

It was that terrible army who had set up the beasts to be in that cave. It was a trap the army had set up to catch the Travelers, and it was a brilliant plan—that is until the twins wandered into the cave.

Shrailzhar's Army had sent three very hungry guimphars into the cave as soon as they'd seen that Jennifer and Judah had become separated from the others. Oh, the armies were so excited, and of course, they had noticed immediately because that dreadful army never took their eyes off the twins—not even for a moment.

When the wind storms had risen, and the fireballs began falling, and the twins turned and headed into that little shelter while the others kept going straight—the army rejoiced. Until then, they were unsure of how to separate the twins from the rest, but then, as they watched, it just happened. The army didn't have to do anything. The Travelers—oh those foolish Travelers—separated themselves. They just let Jennifer and Judah walk off without even noticing.

The army moved quickly and closed off all the other openings that the remaining Travelers may try and find shelter in … except for one. In that one, they released the miserable guimphars. Now, the guimphars were very hungry since the army had them locked up for days and refused them any food.

The army had arranged a hideous plan just days before the Travelers returned for Winter Solstice, which included the guimphars. They needed them hungry, however, and so the army was able to catch three of the terrible beasts and lock them up. Catching them was extremely difficult and it took a great effort from the army. They wanted to capture at least a dozen, but all they could find were three. One of those three, however, had a nest of hungry baby guimphars waiting, making that one all the more eager to find food.

Keeping food from them for a few days would make sure that, if the opportunity arose, they would gobble those Travelers right down. The only problem that the army had in their otherwise perfect plan was that they had no way to make sure to keep the twins away from the guimphars. They shouted in glee as the Travelers had taken care of that problem themselves.

Now that Jennifer and Judah had wandered into the cave, though, the army began to panic. The king would have their heads if they allowed the guimphars to take the lives of the twins. Shrailzhar had told them specifically to make sure that not even one hair on the twins' heads was injured, and now, here they were, right in the pit of three hungry guimphars.

The army panicked and became flustered. They had no idea how to reverse the trap they'd set. There was one way—feed the guimphars before they feasted on the Travelers. But how? There was only one way in and one way out. The only way they could feed the guimphars was to get between the Travelers and the hungry beasts. That is, if they had not already devoured the Travelers.

Oh, the idea that the guimphars may have already filled their bellies with the flesh of the twins caused a wild commotion among the army. The king noticed and decided to keep an eye on all things in his land. He had the land itself, both the air and sky, the floor and the wind, all under his control. The Nakah Warriors were in place, ready for the upcoming war, freeing the king to direct his attention to the army.

He sat high upon his dragon-looking beast and demanded to know from the Army Chief what the commotion was about. Of course, the Chief was not about to admit they had, in fact, lured the twins right into a trap that was sure to cost them their lives. Certainly not! The king wouldn't have hesitated to bring his sword down; he would not have even cringed at slicing off his own Chief's head.

Therefore, the Chief of the king's army got down on one knee and bowed low before his king and made up a most heinous lie.

"Oh, great and mighty King Shrailzhar—the only one worthy to rule such a marvelous land as Trilleah, the only one worthy to sit on the throne—the commotion of your army is simply a deep anticipation of the War of the Firmament."

The king grinned and lowered his sword a little. Disgusting greenish slime dripped from the corner of his mouth and ran down his black breastplate. The chief of the army saw how he was pleasing the king—and earning his trust—so he continued.

"Please forgive the army for causing such a disturbance, but we are so near to capturing those hideous Travelers that the army can hardly contain its excitement." All the while the chief was feeding the king's unquenchable ego, he remained on his knee with his head bowed low. The entire army had done the same, and that sight alone made the king crazy with power as he saw such a multitude bowing to him.

"Rise Up!" King Shrailzhar bellowed with great pride. "I will overlook the commotion because of your anticipation." The chief stood, but the others remained bowed low, waiting for their chief to direct them. Of course, this only fed the king more. The truth was that the army was simply too afraid to rise up; they knew the truth and were terrified to look directly at the king, lest he saw the lies in their eyes.

"Watch and be ready. Soon you will go and take the heads of those Curse Breakers." And just when the army thought they had avoided the king's wrath, he thrust his sword high into the air and wailed, "BRING ME THOSE TWINS!"

Hungry Guimphars

23

Even though the twins were hidden in the darkness of the cave, they were very busy trying to figure out how to get out of the predicament in which they now found themselves. The others were doing the same, but since nobody could talk to anybody else, finding a solution was difficult.

They still had no idea where all the blood had come from and hoped it wasn't from any of the Travelers, although they didn't know from who else it might be. Nobody knew whether to whisper or to speak at all, or if they should be hiding or maybe even running in one direction or another. It was impossible to figure such things out in the dark silence.

Pierce was the one who was closest to the whimpering of what had been so close to him just moments earlier, so he knew to remain quiet. He turned directly around and faced Bella. It was the first time in a long while that he was not feeling the wretched breath of the unknown creature on his face.

He held his hands out and found Bella straightaway. He moved closer to her face and whispered, "I don't know what to do." That was the first time, in all the journeys they'd been on, that she had heard him admit weakness, and the first time she heard the fear in his voice. He had always made such a great effort to hide his feelings.

Mostly, he hid his feelings because he was trying to gain Bella's trust, but also because he wanted to be in charge. A good leader should be the one without fear, after all.

That was precisely what Bella had thought all along. She was partly right; Pierce did want to gain Bella's trust. He had a great liking for the girl from the first moment he'd seen her. Bella was indeed very beautiful and it was impossible not to notice her sweetness.

Sure, she had perfectly straight blonde hair that glistened and shone like the sun, and bottomless blue eyes. Oh, those eyes. When Pierce looked into Bella's eyes, he felt like he could swim the deepest oceans or climb the highest mountains. When he looked into her eyes, he felt like there was nothing he could not accomplish. But now, that confidence couldn't be found whether he could see her or not.

She had the skin of a princess. It was ivory and flawless. Pierce knew it was flawless because he stared at it longingly every time he had the chance. She smelled wonderful all of the time, no matter what. Whether they had just made the long journey to Trilleah or if they were in a pit or a cave or running from fireballs or being spit at by Leviathan, Bella smelled delightful.

Her lips were like the fresh blooms of springtime roses, and he had dreamed more times than he could remember about how soft they would feel against his own.

Even with all of those stunning features, it was her heart that made her perfect. Her heart shone and peeked out every time she opened her mouth. Whether she was scolding or encouraging him, Pierce's skin tingled every time she came near and his heart beat faster each time she spoke his name.

But now, he was sure Bella would lose all hope in him. After all, she had trusted *him*, not Matt, and had asked *him* to lead them into the caves. He thought for sure she must feel the same way about him that he felt about her, but if she had felt that way previously, she wouldn't feel that way anymore. He was certain she would hate him now.

He wanted to come up with some amazing plan to rescue her and the others, but it was his fault they were here to begin with. It wasn't his Shailma who had led him here at all, it was the dark voice he'd let into his heart. If he could sacrifice himself to rescue the others, he'd be willing. Well, he thought he'd be willing, but if the opportunity was given to him, he wasn't completely sure he'd take it.

"Bella," he whispered, "I'm so sorry. I led us in here and now there's no way out." He felt her cheek with the tips of his fingers and feared his eyes might never be able to look upon the one he loved again, and it would be all his fault. "I am so sorry."

If Bella could see into the dark, if suddenly a light was to pop on, she'd have lost all confidence in him instantly. If she had been able to look into his eyes right now, in this very moment, she would have seen into Pierce's heart and would not have liked what she found there.

But she couldn't, so she had no idea he was looking at her with hungry eyes—eyes that would cause a shiver to run through her blood. Of course, it wouldn't have been Pierce's eyes she'd have seen at all, but the eyes of the Dark One instead.

"Oh Pierce, you didn't lead us anywhere," she scolded. Even in her scolding, his heart beat faster when he heard his name roll off her tongue. "There was nowhere else for us to go. We needed shelter and this is what was available," she whispered.

"I have been speaking with Shura, and I'm having trouble hearing him. I don't know why, but I need to get back and talk to the twins." Of course, the reason she could not hear Shura clearly was that her mind was very busy trying to keep the panic from taking over. There were many reasons to panic here, but of course, being Bella, she thought it was her job to keep everyone else calm and never let anyone know how afraid she was.

The truth was not, in fact, that she needed to get back to speak with the twins about the predicament they were in because she never thought for one second that either Jennifer or Judah had any more wisdom than she did. The truth was that she needed to get back to her niece and nephew because she was sure the end was near for them all.

Bella saw no possible way out of this mess and so when it all ended, she wanted to be with Jennifer and Judah … and Matt.

"Go," Pierce said. He wanted her beside him, of course, but knew he needed to tell her what she wanted to hear and so he did. "Bella, we're going to be okay." He knew that was a big fat lie, but he was trying to be very brave for her sake. "We are going to get out of here. Don't you worry, I'll get us out."

He wanted to believe it, he really did. But inside, just beneath his sweating damp skin, he didn't believe a word of it—neither did she.

Bella took Pierce's face between her hands. She got up on her tiptoes, leaned in close, and kissed him on the forehead. It was covered in sludge from the spewing of whatever beast had been wheezing at them, but she never minded. She fully believed this would be the last opportunity to do so and she took it.

Without saying another word, Bella wiped the sludge from her face and turned around. She felt for Kaija Mae.

"Kaija Mae," she whispered softly.

"I'm here," Bella heard back.

"I need to get back to the twins. Help me squeeze by you." Kaija Mae moved as far as she could and directed Bella past her. Kaija Mae squeezed Bella's hands before letting her go back to Tahlia, who was the next in the line.

One by one, Bella wiggled and squeezed her way past every Traveler. She had a few soft, comforting words for each; she kissed the foreheads of the ones she knew well and squeezed the hands of the ones she didn't.

Finally, she reached the spot where Aviel was still holding Sam. Bella didn't realize Sam had passed out and she put her face beside him. She whispered a few things to him, although he couldn't hear her, of course. That made no never mind to Bella, though, and she continued to tell him how proud she was of him and how lucky she was to know such a brave young man. She leaned in close until her lips were touching his ear.

"Sam," she whispered, "Justice will be okay. We will find that last tablet and break the curse of the Waiting Ones. Justice will be free, Sam, because of you."

The boy didn't stir.

Bella felt for his neck and put her fingers where a pulse should be. "Please let me feel something," she whispered. "Please, please." She was holding her breath, terribly afraid there would be no pulse, and no blood flowing through Sam's veins. After a long few seconds, she felt a *thump, thump,* in his neck and breathed a relieved sigh. "Thank you," she mumbled.

She kissed him on the cheek and squished her fingers through his wonderful hair one last time. Bella stood up and realized she'd made it to where Matt stood.

"Matt," she whispered.

"Bella," he whispered back.

Oh, she loved him, indeed she did. He was the most handsome man she'd ever laid eyes on. He was kind and thoughtful and sweet and strong and oh, such a gentleman. Bella felt completely safe with him and trusted him completely. Matt was the one person she'd been able to confide in, both in Trilleah and back home in Westlock.

Nobody else had known, but Matt did not live all that far away from Westlock. He and Bella had seen each other often and most recently, just before this last journey, they had planned to spend the holidays together. In fact, that was the secret she had planned to surprise the twins with, but instead, they were brought here—to Trilleah.

Matt and Bella had spent long hours talking, but now she didn't know what to say to him; partly because there is simply no "right thing" to say in such a bleak circumstance, and partly because the twins were so close. She could hear them chattering back and forth just a few inches away, but Bella couldn't just pass by Matt and say nothing.

Oh, of course, she needed to be with the twins, there was no doubt about that. But she also knew Matt was back here—at the back— and she wanted very much to be with him. Especially if the end was about to come, she wanted to be in Matt's arms, not Pierce's.

"Bella," Matt whispered. "I heard you coming," he said. "I don't know if there's any way out of this." He found her tiny, cold hands and held them firmly in his big, strong ones. She'd always admired his hands. They looked like they could do anything. She thought probably, if he could get those hands on the beast that was in this cave, he could rip it to shreds and save them all. She had no doubt about such things when it came to Matt.

Bella had watched his hands many times; noticed them. The first time he came to Trilleah and had carried the dishes from the Eating Chamber back to the kitchen and washed them, she'd noticed his gentleness. Matt was so strong and gentle all at the same time—it was probably one of those times when Bella had fallen in love with him.

That was why she had given the tablets to him to carry this morning. She knew they were fragile, but they would be safe in Matt's hands. Now, as she thought about it, she wondered where they were.

"Matt," she whispered, "where are the tablets?"

"Judah has them," he replied.

Bella was relieved. She knew he must have given them to someone when he was helping Sam, but she hadn't thought about it until just now when his hands were filled with hers instead of the tablets.

Matt transferred Bella's left hand and now held both of her hands in his right one. With his left hand, he felt her face and noticed her cheeks were damp. *With tears*, he thought. He moved his face close to hers; so close in fact that his lips were touching her cheek.

"Bella," he whispered.

She could feel his lips move on her cheek and his breath was sweet and warm.

"We'll be okay," he said.

"I know," she answered back. Even though she doubted the words Matt spoke, not for one second did she doubt the one who spoke them. There was nothing in her that believed they would ever get out of this cave. As Matt leaned in to kiss her, a loud boom ricocheted off the walls and was deafening. It caused the cave to shake and the hearts of those inside to panic.

Matt pulled Bella behind him, causing her to bump into Judah.

"Judah," she whispered and grabbed him tight. "Jennifer, where are you?" she called softly. Bella let go of her nephew with one arm but held on tightly with the other. She waved and wagged her free arm around desperately trying to find her niece.

"I'm here, Auntie," Jennifer spoke as her own waving arms found Judah and Bella. The three of them clung together in the dark, just behind Matt, and hung on tightly while the biggest of the unseen beasts growled and roared loudly … and hungrily.

Crumbling Caves

24

The king shifted his attention back to the skies. There was so much for him to keep an eye on, but he was king, after all, so of course, he was able to be aware of many of Trilleah's activities at once.

He could not see everywhere at the same time, though. If he could, he'd have killed every one of those miserable Curse Breakers himself long ago. He couldn't see that the Travelers were trapped inside the one cave that his armies had not closed off or the brilliant trap that had been set up inside. He couldn't see there were three guimphars trapped in the same cave—thanks to his army—and he certainly could not see that the twins had mistakenly been lured deep into the trap.

King Shrailzhar trusted his army to make sure those twins were put safely into his hands, so it was a good thing for his army that he was unaware of the danger into which they had allowed those two to wander.

Oh, the plans King Shrailzhar had for the two of them; especially that loathsome girl. That one, in particular, had caused the king so much trouble; nothing but grief! Every time the king thought he had her in his hands, she'd slip right through his fingers and escape— usually with another one of his clay tablets.

Oh, how he despised her.

Most recently, King Shrailzhar had come up with what he was sure would be the perfect plan. He would hide one of the tablets in his very own lair to try and lure her in. It had worked brilliantly. He used the vines to trick the Travelers into leading her right into the center of his trap and then, once she was there, in the exact spot he'd set for her, those vines reached up and ripped her from the grip of her friends.

Of course, they were not vines. They were really thousands of his dark adders, but they were disguised so well that those stupid Travelers saw precisely what the king wanted them to see; a vineyard.

Yes, he was certain he had her that time.

The king had paraded all those weary shells of the Waiting Ones in front of her, trying to wreck her completely. He even used her own mamma to persuade the girl to remain in his pit. It nearly worked, too. He nearly had her right in his hands, except for his stupid dragon. Oh, that stupid swine refused to move close enough for the king to grab her. He had no idea what was wrong with that stupid dragon, but the king would have none of it.

King Shrailzhar always had the last say in such matters, however, and the very next day he took that beast out, chopped off his head, and fed his brains to the garvens. No creature that was fortunate enough to carry the great King Shrailzhar would disobey him and get away with it. How dare he! When would these dragons of the land—his land—realize that he would not tolerate disobedience?

Anything or anyone that dared to come against the great king of Trilleah would most certainly meet a quick and painful end. He would put their heads on a pole in the hot sun for a reminder to the others not to cross him. He was despicable.

Shrailzhar snapped back to the present. He jerked his head around to see where the sudden quivering was coming from. Somewhere in the land, there was a shaking. It was slight and hardly noticeable from where the king was standing, but nothing got by him; not in this land … not in his land!

Pierce shrieked. Whatever had wounded that last beast, the one that had slinked back whimpering, had finally moved right up and was straight in front of Pierce's face. There was no quiet rumbling growl from this one. There was only deafeningly loud howling, roaring, and clawing. Pierce could hear his claws ripping through the ground right in front of him. His imagination saw what must surely be razor-sharp claws coming from whatever deplorable creature this was.

"SOMEONE PICK UP SAM …" Pierce wailed. "And RUUUN!"

There was no point in being silent anymore; that beast knew the Travelers were there. Pierce hoped that Matt heard him, but he couldn't wait to find out.

Kaija Mae was right behind Pierce, and when he turned to hurry the others back out the way they had come in, he picked her up and kept right on going. He didn't know who it was he'd grabbed, but it made no difference. If he could have carried them all out, he would have if it meant moving faster.

He could feel the hot breath of this beast spewing and puffing on his neck and he could hear the teeth snapping. For just a minute, Pierce was thankful it was dark. Hearing and feeling whatever was behind him was horribly terrifying, but seeing it would have made all things so much worse, if that were possible.

Surely he would have fainted dead away. He'd heard of people who died from fear and he anticipated being one of them very soon.

The roaring that was coming from this creature was piercing to the ears. Pierce and Kaija Mae's ears were vibrating and their heads were pounding. They couldn't tell yet, that the walls and roof of the cave were also vibrating from the loud roars, but they couldn't miss the fact that the floor was shaking beneath their feet.

This shaking was what the king was feeling, and this is exactly where he was headed. "HiYah!" he howled to his dragon and kicked his boots hard into its sides. The beast bucked hard and took off like a shot.

"The roof's gonna cave in!" Matt hollered. He and Aviel were struggling to drag Sam along without touching his wound or letting his arm bang into the walls. He was so tall, much taller than either of the boys who were trying to carry him, and doing all this … at top speed … in the dark … was excruciating.

There was not even a sliver of light to see anything. More than once, Matt stepped on the heels of whoever was in front of him and more than once, he heard a loud "OUCH." But slowing down was not an option so the ones in front would just have to speed up.

Sure enough, dirt and pebbles and rocks began raining down from above the Travelers.

"OUCH," Judah hollered.

"GO FASTER!" Aviel screamed.

There was no way to go faster. The girls were in front and it's ridiculous to run as fast as you can run in the dark with rocks jutting out from the sides and the roof falling. There's just no way to do such a thing "faster."

They did their best, though. Bella had her arm out to the side with her hand feeling the edges of the cave on her right, and Judah had his arm out with his hand feeling the side of the cave on his left. Jennifer was in-between, holding tightly onto their free hands that were not feeling along the walls. It was crowded to move that way and they couldn't run at all, but they figured it was the best and safest way to go.

If rocks jutted up from the ground and one of them tripped, the other two would hold them up. If large or sharp rocks were sticking out from either side, Judah or Bella could shout back to Aviel and Matt so they could avoid them. There was just no better way to go. If they moved too quickly and toppled over, the others behind them would surely topple as well until they were one big pile of supper for this hungry beast that was now right behind them.

The only fortunate part was that the beast chasing them was enormous in size, forcing it to move slowly. It couldn't run at all but instead had to squeeze itself through the cave on every step. It spent more time clawing at Pierce than actually moving toward him. But in such darkness, one could never be aware of such fortunate things, so the Travelers had no idea.

Pierce was shrieking. The others thought he was trying to hurry them, but the truth was that he was feeling the tongue of whatever was chasing them, on the back of his neck. His hair was dripping wet with sludge and saliva from that beast.

Pierce could hear that thing panting and growling, but the gnashing of its teeth was so close that he was certain he might lose his head at any moment. More than once Pierce was sure the claws of the beast had hooked on his jacket.

"FASTER!" he shrieked again. The others tried to move faster, but they were already going as fast as they could. There was no way they could go any faster. The passageway was overflowing and echoing and shaking with the sounds of shrieks and hollers and cries and wailing.

But suddenly …

Bella's hand that she had been dragging along feeling the edges of the wall, unexpectedly now felt nothing. The wall ended. She could tell it wasn't the exit; if it were, there would have been light peaking in and that was certainly not happening. In fact, there was still not even a sliver of light, which told her they were nowhere near an exit.

She knew this was a different passageway altogether because when they entered such a long while ago, they had gone straight the entire time. Bella knew this for certain because when they came into this cave, she had been walking at the front with Pierce and they discussed how one cave could go on and on for such a great distance without having any turns or curves or twists or passageways.

Bella knew for absolute sure that this passageway was not here when they came in, or they somehow had missed it.

Without having any time to think or talk it over with the others, she turned and yanked Jennifer's hand. Jennifer pulled on Judah, and they all hurried into the passageway to the side. Now, the twins had learned the lesson very well that when you're in front of several others and you turn off, they may not follow you; especially if they can't see you. That was exactly how they had gotten separated the last time.

They made sure to avoid such a conundrum this time.

Judah held his arm out, blocking the ones behind him and screamed, "THIS WAY!" His flailing arm finally flung into someone's chest, and he grabbed the shirt of whoever it was. It was Aviel. He, Matt, and of course, Sam, who remained unconscious, followed Judah.

Just a few steps into this much smaller passageway, it became so narrow they were forced into a single line, slowing them down significantly. Nevertheless, Pierce kept right on screaming and trying to push the others. It was no use; they could not move any faster.

The passageway they had turned into shrunk smaller and smaller until they were forced to drop to their hands and knees and crawl through the dirt. Pierce had quit screaming, and in fact, they had not heard a sound from him for quite a few, very long minutes now. There was no growling or roaring from the beast either, and the others hoped that they had lost him. There was certainly no space for wild beasts of any kind down this very dismal passageway, so likely, it had carried on down the bigger space.

The Travelers were so focused on trying to keep going forward that they didn't think anything of Pierce's sudden silence; they just kept on going. Some of the spaces were so small that the bigger boys had to squirm through on their bellies and were grunting and groaning as the rough ground tore through their skin.

Pulling Sam through the passageway was exhausting, tedious, and slow. Maneuvering the unconscious boy required Aviel on one side and Matt on the other, for a good portion of the way. Jennifer was quite far ahead, just behind Bella, and had not yet realized that Sam was unconscious. With so much screaming and hollering and roaring, it was hard to know what was going on at all. Her only focus was getting out of the cave before it collapsed upon them, becoming their graves.

Jennifer was nearly unable to breathe, for a deep fear had gripped her. All she could think of was that they had crawled right into the beast's food dish and if the land quivered even slightly, they would be squished like bugs before they even realized it. There were so many fears running through Jennifer's head that she was nearly immobilized. Her imagination went crazy and she envisioned falling right into a huge bowl with all the starving beasts there waiting for dinner to be delivered.

"LOOK!" Bella screamed. They couldn't look, of course, because the passage was so small that if they did look, all anyone would see was the one right in front of them.

"What is it?" Matt replied. "We can't see …"

"LIGHT!" she screamed again. "There's light up ahead! I can't see where it's coming from, but there is definitely light. This must be the way out!" Judah hollered.

Hearing Bella holler about seeing the light, no matter how small, calmed Jennifer a little—enough to put her imagination on pause and have her move quicker. No need to tell her to hurry now, for she was hurrying. Her knees were bleeding, she was sure from crawling on the hard rocks, but probably everyone else's were as well. That was not something she was going to complain about … if they ever got out of here.

And they would get out, she knew it now. The light was breaking through more and more with every step that passed. Their breathing became more relaxed; their minds became slightly calmer. Pierce had stopped his shouting and was quiet, but nobody paid much attention. They figured that whatever had been trying to fill its belly with their flesh was much too big to follow the Travelers into this tiny passage and had given up. Surely, that was the reason Pierce had calmed down.

They were wrong.

They wouldn't realize it, however, until each and every one of them had dragged themselves out of this horrible cave and were standing on the other side with lights of the sky beaming down. Once they were out, once they had checked Sam thoroughly to make sure he'd survived being dragged through a long passage of rocks, then they would realize it.

Then they would see that they came out of the cave cut and bleeding and dirty, and that one of them had come out unconscious and clinging to life, and that one had not come out at all.

Seeing is NOT Believing

25

The Travelers were nearly out of the painfully undersized cave. They could finally see an opening at the end, although it was very tiny. Well, Bella could see it since she was at the front, but nobody else could see past her. The opening was so tiny that they were going to have to chip out much of the rock to squeeze through. Nevertheless, it was going to lead them out, back into the Dark Land, which did not look as dark as it had been when they'd entered the cave.

Bella was the one who was going to have to do the chipping away of the rock because she was the one at the front. She was the only one who could reach the hole so it would have to be her; there were no other options. They had found a way out and had finally escaped the grip of that beast who wanted to enjoy them for his lunch.

"Can you go any faster, Bella?" Matt asked gently. He was not trying to pressure her or suggest she wasn't doing enough to get them out. He was, however, getting very concerned for Sam. The unconscious boy's breathing was slowing down and then speeding up, and Matt knew he'd lost a lot of blood. Matt didn't say anything about his concerns for Sam to Bella, though, not right now. He didn't want to upset the girls.

Jennifer had not yet become aware that it was Sam's blood they'd seen—Sam's blood that had led them into the very cave that they were still trying to get out of. She would know soon. There was so much else on her mind that she'd forgotten all about the pools of blood her and Judah had seen outside.

There was much that the twins would find out straightaway, and much they would tell the others. But first, getting out of this tight space was their priority. They had finally reached the small opening where a glimmer of light had been poking in, and now they had to make it just big enough to squeeze through.

"I'm going as fast as I can," Bella called back. "If I had a knife or a stick or something, it would help. Can anybody find anything that might help me chip these rocks away?" Even as she was hollering, a large chunk of rock came down and landed on her hand. "Ouch!" she whimpered.

"Here," Aviel shouted and tried to hand a pocket knife up to Bella.

"You've had this the whole time?" she asked. She sounded annoyed, but there was no time for reprimanding anyone. Bella just took the knife and continued chipping away.

"I forgot about it until you asked," Aviel said. "Sorry, Bella."

In what seemed like a long while, Bella had chipped away enough of the rock and hard dirt to squeeze herself through. "Should I go through or keep chipping?" she asked the others. "Only Jennifer and I will be able to fit through this hole."

Judah answered straightaway, mostly because he wanted his sister and his aunt out of this cave just in case the land began shaking again and the cave gave way. He didn't think it would since he was sure the War of the Firmament had already been fought—and won—but still, he wanted the girls on the other side of this cave as soon as possible in case it crashed down, burying whoever was left inside. It felt a lot like he'd imagine a coffin to feel, so if he could get Jennifer and Bella out, he'd feel a little relieved.

"If you can squeeze out, Bella, do," he said. "Jennifer, you too."

"Leave the knife so we can keep chipping our way out," Matt added. Bella looked around to see if there was a good spot to leave the knife. She supposed she could take it through and then hand it back, or perhaps even keep chipping away from the other side, but truthfully, her hands were aching. It seemed as though she'd been banging and picking away for a long time, and the rocks kept falling onto her hands.

She could find no good space to tuck the knife, so she tossed it out of the hole and began squeezing herself through. Bella quickly popped out the other side, but not without many scrapes and cuts. Her clothes were torn, but she didn't care; she barely noticed. She turned back to help her niece squeeze through.

Jennifer was able to scurry right through for she was quite a bit smaller than her auntie. Bella grabbed the knife and handed it back inside to the boys. They began chipping away frantically. Bella thought they were panicking far more than she had been, but she didn't realize it was because of how bad off Sam had become.

Matt had to get Sam out of there … and fast. He had quit breathing a couple of times, but Aviel had given him some of his own breaths. Nobody knew how bad off Sam was except for Matt and Aviel; that was the very reason they were chipping away like madmen on that rock opening.

Bella took a minute and gawked around the land. She couldn't believe what she was seeing! When they had taken shelter in the cave—a long while ago—the land was in crisis. The winds had been so strong, throwing fireballs and lightning, that the Travelers could barely stand. It was so wretched, in fact, that they hadn't realized the twins had turned off and headed a different direction … until it was too late.

Remembering that they had been separated from the twins for so long, Bella gave Jennifer an enormous hug and a sappy kiss on the cheek. Jennifer looked at her like she had lost her mind, and maybe she had. Jennifer realized she had no idea how long the others had been trapped in that cave before she and Judah had found them. She threw her arms around her auntie and squeezed tight.

Bella smiled down at her niece and continued turning her head this way and that, taking in all the unusual sights of Trilleah. Looking around, she saw the land was completely still. Peaceful almost. The sky caught her eye as the most beautiful sky she had ever seen, and it caused her to gasp.

Jennifer noticed Bella's reaction and realized the other Travelers would not have known about the land's calmness.

"What happened?" Bella asked. Her eyes were large as she was searching across the land, taking in all the sights she'd never seen here before; not in Trilleah.

While the boys continued chipping away at the rocks, Jennifer began to explain about the War of the Firmament and that as far as she and Judah could tell, the war was over and they must have won because of all the peace. Of course, if Jennifer would have thought much about what she was saying, she'd have quickly realized the error of such an assumption.

Bella couldn't believe what her ears were hearing. She shook her head and kept looking around. The chipping away of the rocks behind her faded as she stared up at the sky. There was, of course, no way she could know that the beauty she was seeing was only a reflection of something else … something else purely and thoroughly and consumingly dreadful.

"What are those piles of black ash?" she asked Jennifer, as though Bella thought Jennifer must know which, of course, she didn't.

"I don't know," she answered. "They weren't here when Judah and I were looking for you." And then, as Jennifer considered all the things that *were* there when they were searching for the others, she remembered the blood.

She opened her mouth to ask Bella about it. Still, she didn't realize anything had happened to her dear Sam, but as she started to ask, Jennifer was interrupted by a loud shout from inside of the hole. And then, many shouts. They sounded like happy shouts and the girls immediately dropped back to the ground and peered inside.

"What is it?" Bella shouted.

All the voices started chattering at once, but finally, it was Matt's deep voice that came out of the hole clearly; along with his arm. The girls could not believe it. They were speechless. Jennifer looked at Bella … Bella looked right back at Jennifer.

"LOOK!" Matt shrieked as he thrust his arm out of the hole toward the girls. There, in his filthy, grimy, bloody hand, was a tablet. The last tablet. They had found it even though they weren't even looking.

No wonder they were hollering like a bunch of silly girls inside that hole. In an instant, Jennifer reached out and gently took the tablet from Matt, and in the same instant, Bella flopped to her belly right in front of the hole and kissed the one whose hand had just passed that tablet through the hole.

Bella didn't care how dirty his face was, or how ruffled up her hair might be. She didn't care that there wasn't time for such things while the others were still stuck in the cave, and she didn't care who saw it. Bella loved the boy and he had just handed them the most valuable possession she could have ever hoped for, and so she kissed him.

He didn't turn red like she suspected he might, although, his face was so grimy and dirty that she wouldn't have been able to tell if it had!

"Matt!" she shrieked, "where did you find this?" The Travelers had been so busy trying to survive that they'd forgotten they had one last tablet to find. But now, there it was, right in Jennifer's hands.

The one thing all of this had been for, that very thing they had ventured to find, that they had endured tornado speed winds and flying fireballs and wild beasts and the Army of Shrailzhar, was now in their possession. They had them all. They finally had them all.

Oh, how Bella jumped and danced and shouted and laughed. Jennifer was already dancing and singing and jumping all around, so Bella joined her. Together they looked ridiculous, but they didn't care, not even a little.

"Auntie," Jennifer squealed as they held hands and danced around, "You kissed Matt!"

"Yup," was Bella's shameless reply. "I did."

They had done it. Those Travelers had found all the clay tablets and the curse of the Waiting Ones could now be broken.

"Oh, Mamma!" Jennifer screamed at the top of her lungs as she looked up at the sky. "We did it, Mamma! We did it!"

Bella was excited as well, but she was trying to hear where Matt had found the tablet, so she hushed Jennifer, who was not exactly happy about it, but she hushed nevertheless.

"I was chipping away at the rocks here," he said, and lifted the knife up toward the rocks to demonstrate, "trying to get a space big enough to push Sam out. The tablet just fell out of the rocks and hit me square in the head!" Matt said. Bella looked at his head and saw he did indeed have quite a red bump and a slight cut just above his left eye.

"You mean to tell me it was hidden in the rocks? The tablet was used to try and block us from getting out?" Bella could hardly believe what she was hearing and it made no sense to her. Her brain suddenly felt scrambled.

Nobody else seemed to think about it for very long; they were all so happy to have the tablet—the last one needed to break the curse. But Bella couldn't get it out of her mind. There was something that was stirring within her now—something confusing and intriguing all at the same time—and she tried to figure it out.

If the last tablet was built right into the cave that had held them for so long, how was it that they'd found it? Who had put it there? How did it get built into the wall? Furthermore, and way more concerning to her, was how they'd found it.

If it was their Shailmas who'd led them to this place to find the tablet, and, of course, it had to be the Shailmas because there is simply no such thing as luck and if there was, then this would have had to be the luckiest thing ever to happen, then it *must have been* the Shailmas who had led them to this cave.

Why would the Shailmas lead them to a cave that had hungry wild beasts inside? Couldn't the creatures have brought them here to the outside of the cave? Did their lives have to be in such danger for the tablet to be found? Surely not, yet there was no other explanation. Her mind was swirling uncontrollably now and the more she let it, the more it swirled. Bella was becoming dizzy and had to sit down.

She was about to become furious with the Shailmas, but before she had a chance, Matt shouted again and they broke through the wall. It seemed that once the tablet was found, the rest of the wall just came tumbling down without any effort whatsoever. It seemed to Bella, who was thinking such deep thoughts about it all, that the tablet was what had been holding the wall together all along.

Out of the Tunnel

26

In just minutes all fury had broken loose. Matt and Aviel carefully and slowly brought Sam through the wall—which was not completely broken down—and held him up until Judah and Bella could kick away most of the rubble and make a smooth place to lay him down.

This was the first time Jennifer had seen him, and it was that very moment when she realized where the blood had come from.

"SAM!" she shrieked and dropped down beside him. She grabbed his unburned hand in her own and began weeping uncontrollably. Her tears fell on his face; great big fat ones. So many tears, in fact, it was like a faucet, landing on his face and washing it clean.

Sam looked dead; Jennifer wasn't sure if maybe he was. He had lost so much blood that his face was white as a ghost—without even a trace of color in his skin except for the bits of blue that had gathered around his lips. They all circled him now; the girls sobbed loudly while the boys were hushed. Tears welled in the corners of their eyes and a few managed to escape here and there. It appeared that Sam would not be making the rest of the journey with them and Justice would have to be freed without Sam's help.

Judah knelt down and gently lifted Sam's grotesquely wounded arm. It had turned a disgusting shade of green and was covered in little pockets of white froth. It smelled horrific.

"This is outrageous," Judah said. His tone sounded angry, but his voice uttered the words with gentleness.

As Jennifer continued to weep over the boy … as her tears continued to splash onto his face, Sam's eyelashes began to flutter. Barely noticeable at first and, in fact, nobody did notice for a time. But then, and quite suddenly, Bella jumped up.

"LOOK!" she shrieked. "HIS EYES!" And sure enough, as they watched Sam's eyes, his long eyelashes continued to flutter more and more.

"He's trying to open his eyes," Kaija Mae whispered. A song stirred within her belly, and as she opened her mouth it immediately started soaring out. She sang loudly. She danced and sang and looked up to the sky.

"THE SKY!" she screamed, for she had not looked up until this very moment. The Travelers were beside themselves with joy and delight at all they were seeing around them. They had not taken even a moment to notice that the land was not the same as earlier—before they ran into the cave for shelter. The beautiful red sky and the calmness of the air struck them as eery, and they were stunned. Never had they seen such color in Trilleah; they would have remembered if they had.

There was not so much as a breath of wind blowing anywhere, not even the slightest breeze. The trees were perfectly still, not even one leaf was fluttering.

But Sam … oh, Sam. Jennifer was still kneeling over him and even though she had stopped her weeping, the tears continued to fall. She couldn't stop them—they had a life all of their own. She gave up trying and just watched them land and roll down Sam's face.

That lifeless face was getting a tiny bit of color back now, and his lips were less blue than before, although his eyes remained closed.

"What are we going to do about his arm?" Judah asked the others. "He can't last like that; the blood is still oozing out of it."

"He can't have much blood left in him," Bella whispered. If Sam could hear them, and now it seemed that maybe he could, she didn't want to have him hear such dreadful things so she spoke at barely more than a whisper.

"Pierce," she said. There was no answer. "Pierce," she called again, slightly louder but still hardly noticeable. She thought maybe he would have an idea about how to stop the bleeding. There was no sign of Pierce anywhere. It was at that very moment—when they were all heading back to the hole in the rock wall to see why he'd not come out yet—Bella's heart was pained and she suddenly had a knowing about why he had stopped screaming earlier, back in the tunnel.

Her mind sped back to that moment and realized that yes, he'd stopped screaming just seconds after they had turned into that last small opening—that tiny place where they had to slow their pace drastically and squeeze in, one by one. It came to her mind also, that was right about the same time they had stopped hearing the growls and roaring of the beast; that one hidden by the dark; that beast none of them had seen, but all of them had heard.

Bella knew; there could be no doubt about it. Pierce wouldn't be coming out of that hole in the rocks. No matter how long the others stood there, or how long they stared inside and waited, or how loudly they shouted to him, Pierce would not be coming out.

The beast had gotten him. It must have. Bella moved quickly to a tree that was standing perfectly still, just a few feet away, and began heaving loudly. There was nothing in her belly to come up, or it would have been spewed all over that tree in seconds. Instead, she felt the painful tugs on her empty stomach as she continued to heave.

Pierce was gone.

She had kissed him on the forehead hours before, wondering if it would be the last time she'd see him. But now, with everyone singing and dancing and rejoicing with the last clay tablet still wrapped in Jennifer's fingers, Bella regretted not saying more to him.

Something …

Anything …

Oh, she regretted every moment that she was cross with the boy and every scolding she'd ever given him.

He was gone.

Bella watched with complete brokenness as the others continued to stare into the hole they'd all just crawled out of. Did they really expect him to suddenly pop out from around the corner? Surely they too must know he'd met his fate between the jaws of that dreadful beast they'd been running from.

Maybe they couldn't bear to accept the truth of what was staring them right in the face. Pierce was gone. He'd sheltered the others—protected them—but it had cost him everything. Did they dare go back inside to find what may—or may not—remain of their dear friend?

"Oh, Pierce," Bella sobbed.

"When will this nightmare end?" She looked up at the red sky, shook her fists at it, and screamed. At the top of her lungs, she screamed. She was so filled with emotion … so twisted up inside. There was fear, dread, anguish, and pure rage at what had happened to Pierce and Sam, relief at what had become of Miriam and then, mixed and swirling with all of that, was sheer delight and excitement at that very thing which Jennifer now held in her hand.

The tablet.

The very reason for all of this. That tablet was the reason they were here in the first place, in this Winter Solstice. They were not supposed to be here at all right now. She and the twins were supposed to be back home on a surprise holiday visiting Matt, but none of that mattered now; not anymore.

"He's opening his eyes," Jennifer squealed and jumped up. She was waving her hands, trying to get the attention of the others. "HEY … Sam's opening his eyes!" she shouted again before dropping back down to her knees. She bent over and put her face very close to Sam's, whispering his name over and over.

"Sam. Sam, it's Jenny," she said softly. Jennifer wiped away her own tears from his face with her sleeve and continued to whisper to him.

"Kaija Mae," she called. "Come sit with us and sing to Sam." It was a good idea, truly it was, but Kaija Mae was having a hard time pulling herself away from the opening in the rocks. Everyone was, except for Bella, that is. She knew Pierce wouldn't be dragging himself from that space. The others knew it too, deep down, but none could make themselves believe it, at least not yet. They refused to believe such a thing and continued calling … waiting … looking.

Pierce had been annoying; that much was true. And often he got on Jennifer's nerves. He had not listened to the others and once in a while, his actions put the rest in dangerous places. But then, more than one time, he had pulled Jennifer to safety and more than one time he had taken great measures to make sure the others were safe, even if it meant that he wasn't.

Jennifer's heart was torn; her head was spinning. She looked toward where Kaija Mae and the rest stood slouched over the opening, waiting and calling for Pierce, and then back to Sam, who was trying hard to open his eyes and say something.

His mouth was trying to move—his lips barely wavering—and he struggled to open his eyes. Finally, Jennifer got angry at the rest who were wasting their time. It was clear that Pierce was not coming out no matter how loud they called him or how long they stood there waiting.

"KAIJA MAE," Jennifer screamed.

They all spun around, startled at the loudness that came from the smallest of them all.

"Please," she begged. "Pierce is not coming out, we all know that. But Sam IS still here—with us—and he needs our help NOW!"

She was right. Even though nobody wanted to admit it, Jennifer was right. They skulked away from the pile of rocks and moved to Sam. None of them spoke; what would anyone possibly say?

"Please, Kaija Mae!" she begged. "Please come here beside me and sing to Sam. He needs your songs."

Simeon, Jennifer searched in her mind. *Make her listen. Make them all listen. Please find Pierce. I know he'll come back to us, I just know it. He has to. Please, Simeon!* She leaned down and kissed Sam's damp forehead and watched as his eyes fluttered again fighting to open.

Kaija Mae did exactly what Jennifer requested. She sat on the ground and began wiping Sam's outrageous red curls away from his face and sang the sweetest song ever to be sung.

"Thank you," Jennifer whispered and tightly held Sam's unwounded hand. Matt gently grabbed his wounded arm and held it up, trying to persuade the blood to stop seeping.

"Open your eyes, Sam," Jennifer begged quietly. "Please … please … open your eyes."

To the King

27

King Shrailzhar was still heading toward the place he suspected the rumbling of his land had come from. He was outraged by it because earlier—immediately after he'd sent the Nakah Warriors out in search of the Shamars—he had clearly instructed every corner of that land to be silent. The land was to remain that way until it heard the four Nakah Generals blasting their horns, signaling the beginning of the War of the Firmament.

That blast had not happened yet. How dare even one tree blow or one pebble fall anywhere in Trilleah. It enraged him. The king and some of his army along with him had ridden a long ways already, but the rumbling only lasted for a very short time, so he wasn't sure which way to go once it had stopped. Now they had paused, and he climbed down from the massive dragon on which he sat. The king picked up a fistful of dirt and spat into it. He rubbed his hands together and then with one great blast of breath, blew hard on the mud ball.

The mud went nowhere but instead, dropped straight back to the ground. The king kicked at it and stomped his heavy metal boot down. He'd forgotten that he had instructed the dirt to remain firm and steady on the ground. So of course, that was exactly where the dirt returned to. It had determined to obey the king, and so it went right back to where he'd scooped it from.

He grumbled under his breath when he saw it. The king was mortified that his usual tricks were not working, but at the same time, he grinned a devilish grin of great pride to know that even the smallest specks of dirt were obeying his commands.

He glanced over to see if his army had noticed, just in case he looked foolish to them. He couldn't look foolish to his army, after all. "Yes … mhm … good then …" he mumbled to himself. On and on he went, being senseless and talking gibberish, noting how perfectly honorable his land was being; all except for the one bit that had rumbled when it was instructed to not rumble.

He climbed back onto the back of his enormous dragon, proud and arrogant. King Shrailzhar sat in the middle of his land and looked around, quite thrilled with himself and looking forward to having the entire land of Trilleah as his own. The entire land—the ground and sky, the trees and sea, and every creature that walked on the ground or flew in the air or swam in that bloody sea—would belong to him for all eternity with no more interference of the Curse Breakers to disturb him.

And the souls. Oh, the souls of the Waiting Ones would finally become the souls of Trilleah. The waiting would be over because they would know their freedom was not coming. The gates of Solstice would be closed and locked, never to be opened again. The curse would cover the entire land and Shrailzhar would be its king for all time.

"To the king of Trilleah," he shouted.

"To the king of Trilleah," his great army replied.

The miserable king threw his head back and laughed. "Ha ha ha." He laughed such an evil laugh that the ground wanted to melt away and let him fall into what it was covering, but it didn't dare.

"Yes," he shrieked. "Once my great Nakah Warriors overtake those dreadful wretched Shamar Shailmas, you shall all be mine and nothing will interfere or come against my Trilleah ever again."

He looked in the direction of where the winds had carried the trees—those that held the souls of the Waiting Ones—and laughed even louder. "And you shall be replanted in the garden that will be prepared for you, right in the center of my land. You shall grow and grow and grow until finally, my entire land will be filled with you. I will have my fill of you all!"

What a brutish and wicked king he was. Even his own land wanted to fade away into the air. Nothing wanted to remain in this place for all of eternity, but especially the souls of the Waiting Ones. Oh, how they moaned now as the brutish king bellowed and shouted. Even though they were far away from where the king was having such a glorious moment with himself, the Waiting Ones could hear him, and they shuddered.

Every tree that contained the soul of a Waiting One shuddered hard, and it should have caused the ground to shake. The ground refused, though, from fear of what the king might do in response to such disobedience.

King Shrailzhar did not even consider that his Nakah Warriors may not win the War of the Firmament. He couldn't. His mind could not even conceive such a thing if, in fact, he had a mind. If the Nakah Warriors could not defeat the Shamars, *and* if his brutish armies could not gain access to the Curse Breakers, *and* if the Curse Breakers were somehow able to find that last tablet and break the curse …

No, the king would not even consider such things.

He knew the results of such an outcome and refused to allow himself to think about that. "We will be victorious," he said quietly to himself. Then just a little louder, "We will be victorious." And finally, that terrible king looked to the sky and raised his sword.

"WE WILL BE VICTORIOUS!" he screamed.

The sky began to shake now, and small rips appeared, revealing the blackness it was hiding.

The Travelers heard something in the air and looked around. They couldn't make out what it was exactly, but there was something making a ruckus just around the bend a few hundred feet away. Some other noise was heard above them, and a couple of the Travelers looked up in search of what it was.

"Look," Aviel said.

Just above them, and a hundred feet to the south and again a hundred or so feet to the west, they saw that the sky had black marks in it. They couldn't tell why, or where the black marks were coming from, but they were certain it wasn't a good thing. It looked like the beautiful red sky was being torn apart. Of course, it would not have ripped and torn so easily if it hadn't already stretched itself so thin to cover up the rips and tears from earlier.

"We've got to get out of this open space," Matt whispered.

"But where are we supposed to go that will be any better?" Bella asked. "It's not as if there are caves or hollows we can hide in. And I'm sure not going back in there!" she stated and pointed toward the cave from which they'd just crawled out.

What a dreadful predicament they found themselves in. If they had known that the king—the very one that wanted their souls—was only a couple hundred feet away from them, just around the bend up ahead, they'd have panicked greatly and happily crawled back into that cave. But so far, they had no idea he was close—or even that he was looking for them at all. In fact, they had assumed that since they had found all the clay tablets, all that was left was to find a safe place to break the curse and this miserable journey would be over.

They were certain the dangers had all passed now, and the Shamar Shailmas had won the war. At the very least, they assumed those Shailmas that Jennifer and Bella had seen earlier were still surrounding them by the thousands and that they were perfectly safe.

"Jen … Jen … Jennifer," Sam squeaked out.

Jennifer whipped her head around since she'd been looking along with the rest up to the sky when Sam had finally whispered her name.

"Sam!" she squealed. "Oh Sam, I thought you were …" she stopped herself before finishing such a bleak sentence. Instead, she leaned down and kissed him again on the forehead. She wiped the red hair from his face and stared into his eyes. They were only half-open, but they were looking right up at her. She'd never noticed what a wonderful deep green they were and the color in those eyes reminded her of the emerald greens back in the Chamber of Rest. She closed her own eyes and went back in her mind, just for a second, to that Chamber.

"Mmmmm," she hummed as she remembered her time there. Was that only this morning? Could that be right? It seemed like years ago. It wasn't just this morning, in fact, it was two mornings ago. Much time had passed since the Travelers left Asphelia's Hollow, but they hadn't realized it.

Without the sun to rise and fall, and with the moon hiding behind the red curtains of the sky, the Travelers assumed this had been one extremely long day. They had no way of knowing anything else.

"Sam," Matt whispered. "How are you feeling?"

I … I don't know," he stammered and stumbled. The poor boy was having a great deal of trouble getting his words out, but that was understandable.

"Maybe don't try to talk," Bella said to Sam. "Just rest." Then she turned to Matt. "Can you keep his arm up? The bleeding has nearly stopped since you've been holding it in the air."

"I can hold it up for a bit longer, but my arms are getting tired. Maybe we can take turns," he replied. Jennifer had not moved from Sam's side; she didn't plan to.

"I'll take a turn," she said and laid the tablet on Sam's chest. Again she leaned down close to his face and whispered something nobody else could hear. "Sammy, we found the tablet. We have them all."

The corners of his mouth turned up, only slightly, but they did turn up nevertheless.

"Do you want me to take that tablet?" Aviel asked. He had the first eleven and thought it should probably be added to them.

"No," Jennifer said. "I think Sam can hold on to it for a few minutes," she added, and winked at the boy who was struggling to keep his eyes on her. She thought she saw a sparkle in those pained emerald gems, but couldn't be sure.

"Sam, you can close your eyes," she said and rubbed his face with the back of her grimy hand. She saw the dried blood on her fingers from where she'd dipped them earlier into the pool just outside the cave. A deep sadness came over her now that she knew, without any doubt, where that blood had come from.

She grimaced as she suddenly wondered if that beast in the cave had left any of Pierce's blood behind; if she'd find a puddle of his blood inside or if maybe, even his blood had been entirely consumed.

Simeon, please! she begged silently. *We need Pierce. He is our leader,* she cried to her Shailma. She had not heard from Simeon for a long while, it seemed, and realized now just how much she missed him. His calm voice came to her mind quickly, as if he had been waiting for her to seek him. She was glad to hear his voice, although she didn't particularly like what he said.

Little One, he whispered to her mind, *Pierce is not your leader. He never was. You are the leader, Jennifer. You are the one who must lead these ones to safety ... and you must do it now.*

But Simeon, she argued, confused. Jennifer was sure the danger had passed, but the words and the understanding she was getting from her Shailma seemed to suggest something different. *Why can't we just wait here for a bit?* Honestly, Jennifer had no idea what they were waiting for.

And then it dawned on her—a thought that interrupted her conversation with Simeon and wound her mind up tight with excitement. She turned to the others and spit out the words that suddenly made more sense to her than anything had ever made sense to her before.

"WE HAVE ALL THE TABLETS!" she screamed.

She heard Simeon trying to get her attention but ignored him for the time being. This sudden understanding that had come to her seemed far more important than anything Simeon might have to say. She had known it in her mind, but suddenly, her heart understood it.

"Yes, Jelly Bean," Judah said.

"We do," added Bella. They were looking at her like she had two heads. She couldn't imagine why anybody hadn't thought of this before now and she couldn't believe that as she was pointing it out, still nobody seemed to get it. Simeon tried again to get her attention and again she talked right over him, ignoring his callings.

Jennifer carefully handed Sam's painfully burned arm back to Matt and jumped to her feet and said it again; slowly.

"We … have … all … the … tablets. ALL … the tablets."

"Are you okay?" Aviel asked.

Jennifer looked around the group of confused Travelers, from one face to the next. Finally, it was the quiet and weak voice of Sam, from the place he was laying on the ground, who spoke up.

"We can break the curse," he whispered.

Nobody said a word for a long time. They just looked at one another, afraid to even believe what Sam had just said, but of course, he had spoken the truth. The truth they had all forgotten was the very reason they'd ever journeyed to Trilleah in the first place. They had been so focused on collecting the tablets, that they'd forgotten the very reason WHY they'd been collecting them in the first place.

This entire time Simeon had been trying to break in and get the attention of the one who should have been listening to him all along. Finally, Jennifer shouted at him.

Simeon, what is it? she demanded.

For the first time, Simeon spoke out loud for every ear to hear. Nobody moved a muscle or breathed a breath because never before had a Shailma spoken in the midst of a crowd. Now that one had, the words were startling.

Jennifer immediately wished she would have listened to her Shailma the first time he tried to tell her because now, it seemed too late.

"The king is coming," he whispered. "The king is coming."

Not by Might

28

The king was coming!

He had heard something just around the bend, so that's where he was heading. Of course, that, "something" he'd heard was the Travelers squealing and shouting as they celebrated over the realization that they had in their hands all they needed to break the curse of the Waiting Ones.

What a celebration it was. They had cause for it, without a doubt, but it was just too loud and they'd tipped off the king as to their location. Of course, King Shrailzhar did not know that it was those very dreadful Travelers who were making such a ruckus in his land.

He didn't realize it was those very ones that he'd set up an entire war to capture. And here they were right around the bend—right in front of him—easily within his reach. Shrailzhar would know soon, though, because he was only a few feet from reaching that bend and he was moving quickly. The only thing separating King Shrailzhar from the Travelers was that one slight bend in the road.

"HiYah," he demanded of the dragon that carried him.

"What do you mean?" Jennifer called out to the Shailma she couldn't see. "Simeon, how is the king coming?"

"Jennifer, I thought you said the war was over and the king had been defeated," Bella cried.

"How can a defeated king be coming for us?" Matt asked, horrified. As their questions echoed, they all realized at the same time that Jennifer and Judah had been wrong. Very wrong. Dangerously wrong. Maybe even deadly wrong.

Simeon! Jennifer moved to the privacy inside her mind and searched for her Shailma like never before; she had been so sure the war was over.

What was all that before, then? Why did the land turn so horrible? Where did that hurricane wind come from? Why did we have to find shelter if that was not the war? She had a thousand and one questions coming to her now, and she rambled off as many as she could before Simeon interrupted her.

Jennifer, hush, he stated firmly. *Listen carefully because your time is limited and you must listen!* She hushed … she listened.

The War of the Firmament has not even begun. It is yet only being prepared for. You will know without a doubt when it has started; you won't need to ask or wonder. You will know. What you saw earlier, two days ago, was the land rising. Trilleah knows more than you, Little One. Trilleah knows the war is about to begin because it sees the Nakah Warriors have surrounded its skies.

You cannot see what's going on and I cannot open your eyes to show you. Jennifer, if you could see what was happening in the atmosphere, you would faint dead away because it's far too powerful for you to witness. That is the reason your eyes have been shielded and I have been instructed not to open them.

But now the king has heard you and the others rejoicing when you found the last tablet. He doesn't know it was you yet, but he knows something is out of control here; he's coming to punish it. He is nearly upon you.

Jennifer, pick up Sam and get back into the cave. I will roll a large stone in front of it so the king and those he's traveling with will go right by. Stay there until I tell you it's safe to come out.

"GO NOW!" Simeon said for all the Travelers to hear and then, the Shailma was quiet.

Jennifer had no more questions swirling in her head because she was in shock. She would have easily allowed herself to freeze with fear except for Simeon's last instruction to go. He said it loudly, for every ear to hear, because if he'd only spoken it to Jennifer, she wouldn't have had the courage to go anywhere.

"Go where?" Judah called out.

Jennifer shook her head hard and then quickly repeated the instructions that Simeon had written on her mind.

"Boys!" she hollered. "Get Sam and follow me!" Judah, Aviel, and Matt carefully helped Sam to his feet while the boy winced and cried.

"Be careful," he begged. "Please be careful."

They were as careful as they could be, but they were also moving quickly. They had no idea what was going on. All they knew was that an unseen voice which they still didn't know belonged to Simeon, had come from somewhere behind the veil of the air and told them the king was coming and to, "Go now."

"Jennifer, what's happening?" They asked her because she seemed to be the only one who knew what "Go now," meant. She'd gone from a regular skin color to ashen white; they had watched as the color drained from her face. Furthermore, Jennifer was the one who'd told them to pick up Sam. It was clear she had more information than they did, so they listened to her now.

"That voice you heard was Simeon," she blurted out. "The king is nearly upon us and we have to move now or it will be too late. Please ..." she begged, "I'll explain later but please, please follow me. Quickly!"

Jennifer was heading straight back to the cave they'd just escaped from and nobody, including Jennifer, wanted to climb back inside. What they wanted, however, did not matter and so she stood at the side of the broken-down opening in the dark cave wall and waved her arms around, trying to herd the others in quickly.

"Get Sam in," she whispered. "Hurry, he's coming!" They could hear the king's horrible raspy voice screaming at those he'd brought with him now, and by the sounds of it, he was just about to come around that bend just down the way.

They could all hear his voice and it spurred them to move quicker. Judah climbed through the rubble and then turned back to get ahold of Sam. The others helped him through.

Once he was safely inside, the others jumped or fell or squeezed in right after him. Jennifer was the last one outside of the cave, and as soon as the moment presented itself, she stuck her leg inside.

"Hurry," Judah hollered.

"Come on, J," Bella squealed.

None of them knew Simeon was going to close off the hole so the king wouldn't see them. They figured they'd have to squeeze themselves back through the tiny passageway far enough inside that the king couldn't get to them.

As she squatted down to duck inside, something caught her eye over in the dirt where Sam had been laying. A flash of heat shot through her body. She squinted and then, realizing what it was, cried out.

"NOOO!" she wailed loudly.

Nobody knew what was happening because they couldn't see past Jennifer. They figured she'd been spotted by King Shrailzhar and so they grabbed her, trying to yank her inside.

SIMEON, she screamed in her mind. *SIMEON, THE TABLET!*

Before she gave her Shailma even a second to direct her, Jennifer wiggled free of all those hands that were grabbing and pulling on her. She swung her leg back out of the cave and ran toward the tablet.

"JENNIFER," they were all shrieking and crying out. "WHERE ARE YOU GOING?"

Everyone was shouting at her now; she didn't hear them. All she could think about was that tablet; the one last tablet. It must have fallen off of Sam's chest when the boys helped him up. Nobody had noticed. As she moved toward it, Pierce came to her mind. She suddenly missed him very much.

"I've got to get the tablet," she whispered to the air.

The moment she was out of the cave, a large boulder rolled in front of the hole, closing it off. She wouldn't be able to get inside now—even if she could grab the tablet in time. Jennifer was trapped. There was no time to consider such things right now, though. She had to get that tablet.

Jennifer ran like she'd never run before. Just as the king turned around the bend that separated them, she dove through the gravel hitting the dirt hard and landed on the tablet. She saw the king looking at her. She watched his arm hurl a sword toward the sky. She heard the deafening shouts of "SEIZE HER!" roll off his lips.

Her fingers frantically wiggled around in the dirt beneath her until they felt the hard clay of the tablet. That little, uncloaked girl, who was about to be seized by two of the king's warriors, wrapped her fingers around that tablet and shoved it into her sock and yanked her pant leg down to cover it. If they were going to seize her, she would do all she could to keep the tablet hidden from them.

No sooner had she concealed the tablet than she saw the iron-clad arms of the king's men reach down toward her.

"SIMEON!" Jennifer screamed.

As she did, her Shailma amplified her voice a thousand times, and it rang throughout the land. It had a painful sharpness to it, and as it ricocheted through the air and echoed from one rock to another and back and forth and round and round, Simeon covered her ears. She felt it. If he had not, the noise that had come from her belly would have caused her to crack and break into a thousand pieces.

At least, that's what it did to the dragons.

The shriek that rung out through the land made those beasts' heads vibrate and their brains scramble. They reared up madly, throwing their riders to the ground. They were thrown so hard that the riders smashed their heads on large jagged rocks. Jennifer hadn't even noticed those rocks earlier, but nevertheless, as those riders banged against them, they were knocked out cold.

The king's dragon-like creature reared up as well, although he was still a long ways off. Shrailzhar saw what had happened to his men and so, not wanting to be caught off guard, and knowing that the Shamar Shailmas were still around, he turned his dragon around and screamed "HiYah!"

Just before the king disappeared back behind the bend, he shouted to the little girl who was shaking and frozen with fear; that one who was face down in the dirt between two of the largest warriors that the king had in his army.

"I'll return for you, Jennifer Lillian Elliot! I'll return with my entire army and I will capture you, and I will lay your brains out in the sun to rot and hang your flesh on a pole for the cradle bugs to feast on. Your soul shall finally belong to me …"

Jennifer had not passed out, although she wished she would have. She heard every word that miserable king screamed at her, and she knew he would be back. Jennifer had no doubt he meant every word he'd just shouted.

She laid there, face down in the dirt, and sobbed quietly. Her tears were soaking the ground and before long, she was laying in mud. Jennifer could hear the ground pounding as Shrailzhar rode away. When she couldn't hear it any longer, she slowly turned her face to the side. Her eyes found one of his guards only inches from her face. He was huge ... absolutely enormous. She knew he was still breathing because she could feel it on her skin.

Jennifer turned her face the other way and saw the second of the guards close by. She was frozen. Fear gripped her so tightly that she couldn't even wiggle her toes. Her breath was hiding and hard to find. She didn't know what to do, or how to do it.

All she heard from Simeon was one word.

Swords.

Swords? she repeated. *What does that mean?* Without moving, she searched for understanding. *Simeon, what does that mean? Is it a secret code? Simeon, help me! These brutes are going to wake up any second now and take me to Shrailzhar ... SIMEON!*

Jennifer, she heard. No matter how worked up and panicked she became, Simeon always remained calm and things were no different now. *Get their swords and take off their heads.*

"NO!" she whispered. "I CANNOT!"

This quiet and timid little girl wouldn't even squish a spider if it was on the sidewalk. She'd walk around it every time or wait for it to move. There was no way she could cut off the heads of these enormous warriors ... no way at all!

Little One, she heard with such compassion from Simeon that she suddenly felt a strange wave of peace roll over her. *I am here with you. I am not asking you to do any of this in your strength but in mine. You must rely on me now, just like you relied on me to move the stone in front of the cave. I will be with you and I will help you.*

Trust me, Jenny. Trust me.

Jennifer took in a deep breath; she felt a sense of power filling her lungs and strength pumping through her veins. She stood herself up and looked at these two over-sized guards. They had to be nine feet tall. She moved to the bigger of the two and bent down to pull out his sword.

Nervously, she laid her hand on it but it wouldn't budge. She put both hands on the ivory handle, jamming her foot against the holder. With all her might, and no doubt a bunch of Simeon's, she yanked and grunted and pulled.

With a horribly slow grinding sound, the sword wiggled and clicked … then slid right out.

If We Must

29

S*imeon*, she cried. *I can't do this!*

But I can, he said calmly.

No sooner had she heard his voice in her mind than her arms lifted over her head and the sword, much too heavy for her to raise in her own strength, was pointing to the sky above the guard's head.

She closed her eyes and nodded to Simeon. "Okay," she said. "If we must." In a flash, the sword came down hard. She shivered fiercely as her arms felt the sword connect with the guard. Jennifer opened one eye, terrified that she'd completely missed and the only thing she had succeeded in doing was making the guard angry.

Peeking carefully through her one open eye, Jennifer saw a swift flow of dark, red blood flowing toward her. In a moment, her shoes were drenched with his blood; his head rolled, coming to a stop right at her feet.

With great sobs and painful gags and heaves exploding from an empty stomach, Jennifer kicked the head away from her foot and ran around to the other guard. Her tennis shoes were squishing with the blood that had filled them and she was disgustingly horrified. All the commotion she was making had disturbed the second guard and he was beginning to stir. Simeon didn't have to tell her what to do now, and he certainly didn't need to persuade her that it needed to be done immediately.

Jennifer moved swiftly.

While she didn't need Simeon to tell her what to do, she desperately needed him to help her do it. The sword was far too heavy for her to raise it up and bring it down with enough force to take the head from the second guard. There was no way Jennifer wanted to fail. She knew it was either his head or hers. One would be coming off shortly, and she certainly didn't want it to be hers!

Jennifer knew she would only get one shot at this. A loud shriek rose from her chest as she raised the sword high above her head. With one more scream and a shout for Simeon, Jennifer brought the sword down hard. She kept both her eyes wide open this time. She couldn't afford to miss her target. She was glad, too, because the guard's eyes popped opened just half a second before his head came off.

If she had hesitated for even a second or had kept her eyes closed, he would have rolled away and overpowered her. More blood flowed freely—so much blood. The floodgates had opened, releasing more blood than Jennifer had in her entire body, she was sure.

Her small hands began shaking uncontrollably. Jennifer let the sword fall into the dirt and immediately bent down to make sure the tablet was still in her sock. It was.

She was alone and alive, but the king would be coming back for her. There was no doubt that King Shrailzhar would be returning quickly with an entire army surrounding him. He had finally found Jennifer and would be back to get her in no time at all. There was nowhere left for her to hide.

Those words that Shrailzhar had screamed out as he rode away came back and filled her mind. His words had gotten to her ears, but she hadn't let them be heard before—when he'd shouted them earlier. But now that the guards were dead and she had the tablet back, the girl had a minute to replay all that had just happened. As she did, Jennifer heard those words loud and clear; they went straight into her soul.

She had no idea what to do or where to go. She was not about to run away, knowing her friends were all inside the cave, so she slumped down to the ground and leaned against the side of the rock. She laid her head just beside the boulder that had sealed the others inside and set out to have a conversation with her Shailma. She concerned herself with many worrisome things like, *What if the stone that you rolled in front of the cave doesn't move?* Or, *What if they can't get out?* And, *They don't have all the tablets ... neither do I. What if I can't get to them or they can't get to me? How will the curse be broken if we can't get all the tablets together?*

Her mind rolled and rattled and sputtered along, filling itself with all sorts of *What If*'s, until she was nearly crazy. Jennifer took the tablet out of her sock and rolled it over in her hands, feeling the inscription under her bloody fingers.

She kicked off her shoes, disgusted at the smell of blood that was seeping from all around her. She gagged and was glad her stomach was empty. Jennifer had never seen so much blood, of course, and for a few minutes she just sat there, squeezing the clay tablet and watching the blood ooze from the two dead guards. It ran downward ... away from the cave. The pale, broken little girl watched as a stream of blood dug its way into the dirt and made a riverbed for itself.

Jennifer was exasperated. She was exhausted and painfully hungry. She had no hope, only dread swaddled her now. Even her fear had nearly run away from her; she wished it would. The only ones who remained beside her were two headless bodies and even they belonged to the enemy.

She sighed, weary, and carefully tucked the tablet back into her sock; Jennifer stood up. There was only one way to see if she could budge this boulder that had been rolled in front of the cave. She placed her hands on it, inhaled deeply, and pushed. Nothing. It didn't budge.

Not even a wiggle … nothing. She flopped down again against the boulder and began to weep.

Inside the cave, the light had been sealed off when the boulder was rolled in front of the crumbled pile of rocks. This seemed far too familiar, and nobody was happy about it. They had no idea why Jennifer had run out, and they couldn't figure out how such a big boulder had blocked them in. Surely Jennifer didn't have the strength to roll it there.

The Travelers, who were again trapped inside the cave, had all been pushing and kicking away at the rock that had managed to roll itself in their way, but so far, they hadn't even made it budge either. Bella was going crazy with fear over Jennifer. They knew King Shrailzhar was on his way to where they were; they'd all heard Simeon's voice say the words. They also knew that Jennifer had forced them to get inside the cave and that she had been trying to get in as well.

"Why would she run out?" Judah asked, bewildered. Of course, nobody had an answer, and nobody could console Bella.

They tried listening to see if they could make out what might be happening on the outside, but the boulder was too big. They couldn't hear a thing.

So there they were; Jennifer on one side of the cave, dreading the moment when the king would reappear around the bend, with the rest of the Travelers on the other side, sure that Jennifer had been captured already. Both sides were trying to figure out a way to move the boulder, but neither side could come up with anything.

But then …

CRAAAAAACK! It sounded like Trilleah had split in two.

Jennifer jumped up, looking around for King Shrailzhar, certain it was he who'd made the sound. Her eyes didn't find him or anything around her or even on the ground. Instead, what she saw was in the sky. An incision had been made in the sky and as she watched, a vicious bolt of lightning came shooting down right toward her.

She jumped back, sure that she was about to get burned up. *Maybe that's how the king is going to do me in,* she thought. Maybe he was such a pathetic king that he couldn't even kill Jennifer himself and had to direct his land to do it for him.

As she was hovering above the ground and shielding her face from the brightness shooting through the sky, she heard an even louder sound just behind her. Immediately, she whipped her head around to see another bolt of lightning as it was thrown down, hitting the boulder. That big boulder cracked right in half and fell away from the cave.

She looked back to the sky where she'd seen it rip open and could not believe her eyes. Jennifer watched the lightning bolt disappear back through the same hole it had come from and the sky pull itself back together, closing completely. Jennifer was transfixed by what her eyes had seen; she stared mindlessly into the sky. She didn't even notice the other Travelers peeking out around the rubble of the boulder.

Matt stepped out cautiously and looked around. He was mortified by what he saw. He didn't notice Jennifer right away because she was off to the far side of where he was looking. Jennifer never saw

Matt because she was so paralyzed by what she had just witnessed that her eyes could see nothing else.

What Matt did see, however, were the two enormous and dead guards. He saw immediately that their heads were nowhere near their bodies and he saw blood ... so much blood. Everywhere he looked there was blood and right there, close to the cave and filled with blood, were Jennifer's shoes.

He screamed. "Jennifer ... NO!" Surely he thought she must have been taken or killed by the king.

When he screamed, he startled Jennifer so badly that she jumped three feet in the air—at least!

"Matt," she called to him, "I'm right here."

She knew it must have been startling for the Travelers to see such a sight and realized the others would likely never believe what she would tell them about the two dead guards. She began to laugh uncontrollably because suddenly, the sight seemed so unbelievable and she knew that it was her who was responsible for the mess. And, of course, a bit of shock had grabbed hold of her.

Now, nobody knew whether Jennifer should go into the cave or the Travelers should come out. However, Jennifer did know that the king would be returning, but for now, he was gone.

Everyone piled out of the cave and listened, not sure whether to believe Jennifer or not, as she rattled off an unbelievable tale of giants and swords and kings and dragons. Every word of that tale was unimaginable, but the evidence of it was right there before their eyes.

They couldn't make themselves believe it; neither could they deny it must be the truth.

The dead and beheaded bodies of King Shrailzhar's guards were there; the bloodied sword was there beside one guard and it clearly had a small handprint embedded in the blood. Then there was the boulder, or what had been the boulder. Now, two broken, jagged pieces were all that remained.

They looked at it carefully and knew there was no way that Jennifer would have been able to roll it in front of the opening. As the Travelers looked closer, they could see exactly where one might think something very hot and powerful had hit that boulder, causing it to crack in two.

Yes, there was evidence to back up everything she was saying, so they had no choice other than to believe her tales.

"But Jennifer," Kaija Mae finally asked softly. "Why did you run out of the cave?"

"Yes!" Bella demanded. "Why didn't you come in with the rest of us?"

Judah added his own list of questions, of course, which concluded with, "What were you thinking, Jelly Bean?"

Jennifer smiled at them all, bent down, and pulled back her bloody sock. When she straightened herself back up, she opened her hand to reveal the reason she had run out of the cave … why she didn't go in with the others … and exactly what she was thinking.

In one moment—with one statement—Jennifer answered all their questions and even the ones that hadn't been asked.

"We forgot the tablet."

The War Begins

30

None of them could believe that Jennifer would take such a risk for the tablet and they all began talking at once. The Travelers sounded more angry than not angry, which was a surprise for Jennifer. Finally, she put her hand up for them to stop since none of them would hush long enough for her to speak. She was far more annoyed with them than they were with her.

"If we didn't get that tablet, the king would have spotted it," she stated harshly.

"Not necessarily, J," Bella argued. "Maybe he wouldn't have noticed it; maybe he would have gone right by it. I'm sure he wasn't looking at the ground."

"Bella, he would have seen it because it had fallen on that smooth space you and Judah made for Sam. He couldn't have missed it!" Jennifer said. Her hands were waving wildly all over the place as she explained her actions to the others. She really couldn't tell if they were angry or relieved or what was going on because while their tones were angry, their expressions looked relieved.

"Well, Jennifer," Matt spoke up in his usual kindness. "I'm sorry you had to be the one to get the tablet, and I'm sorry you had to face all this by yourself." He, too, was waving his hands around. Then he moved toward that little one whom he was so very thankful for and put his arms around her. Matt lifted Jennifer up and swung her around, even though she was such a mess. When Matt set her back down, he had blood all over him, but he didn't care. He took her tiny blood-smeared face in his hands and kissed the top of her head.

"Thank you, Jennifer. Thank you."

She blushed, her face turning the same color as the sky now, and she glanced toward Judah, who had tears in his eyes. "Yes, Jelly Bean," he said softly and wiped his eyes before anyone could notice they were damp. "Thank you."

Suddenly, whatever had been in their questions and their voices, melted away and was replaced with tears and thank you's and kisses and hugs.

That Little One had sacrificed herself without even thinking about it and had been forced to face fears and do horrible things, such as take the heads off the king's guards—all for the last tablet. The tablet they all needed—all of them; not just these ones standing here with such gratefulness of her sacrifice, but all those who were waiting for someone to set them free and release their souls. Yes; they ALL needed that tablet.

"It had to be done," was all she said and tried to change the subject. She was never one for attention, and this was far too much for her. "Now what?" she asked. "Should we take the tablets and find shelter? How do we break this damn curse and get out of this dreadful land? How do I send Mamma's soul to Heaven?"

The Travelers looked at one other, not having answers to any of her questions. They felt reasonably safe at the moment. They each had their Seraphic Shailmas with them as well as about two hundred and fifty of the Shamar Shailmas who'd stayed back to guard them. Of course, none of the Travelers were aware of any of this since all Shailmas stayed well hidden in the atmosphere of the unseen realm. They could sense it, though, more now than ever before.

Now all that was left for the Curse Breakers to do was lay out the dozen clay tablets they'd spent the last few years searching for and break that curse. Some Travelers had been to Trilleah many more times than others and some, like Kaija Mae, Aviel, Tahlia, and a few others, had been in Trilleah almost since it had begun.

But now, with all of the clay tablets in their possession, they only had to figure out how to translate the messages, put them together, and break the curse. It wouldn't be long before the souls of the Waiting Ones would be released and taken into Heaven. This was the easy part … or so it seemed.

The Travelers were getting excited. Jennifer carefully laid the final tablet in the basket with the others. When she saw the two that were broken in half, she was reminded of Miriam. She didn't feel sorry for that girl one bit, but instead, Jennifer was thankful that her tongue would no longer swell up. Jennifer would not miss that Reptilian Mindbender; not at all.

Matt took the basket of tablets and looked at Bella. He raised his eyebrows and nodded at the basket. "Any idea how to break this curse?" he asked. Everyone shook their heads. Nobody had any idea about that, but they all knew what Judah was talking about when he opened his mouth and shared his thoughts.

"If we can lay these tablets out and break the curse before the War of the Firmament begins, the souls of the Waiting Ones will be freed, and the land will be destroyed." He looked at his sister. "Is that right?" he asked.

"I think so," she replied but then hummed for a moment and added, "but I thought the war had already been won so I could be wrong again." She was not wrong, but unfortunately breaking the curse would not be as easy as just chanting some words from an unknown language.

Breaking the curse would require that, for sure, but not only that. They each had very specific keys which would be required to unlock the curse. They didn't know it, of course, for the keys they held were inside of them—not in their pockets or their hands—but in their hearts. Each Traveler was indeed a Curse Breaker and a very necessary part of what was about to take place. They each had been painstakingly and specifically chosen to be here … in this moment … in this land. Much would yet be required of each of them.

The greatest sacrifice of all would yet need to be made by one, and another would have to allow it to happen. Soon, they'd figure out all that would be required from them to free the souls of those they'd been fighting for all this time.

A resounding *BOOOOOM* rang out, shaking the land fiercely and sending them spiraling to the ground. Jennifer immediately looked to Sam, who had been propped up against the wall of the cave.

"I'm okay," he whispered and nodded his head. The bleeding had finally stopped, and they had wrapped his arm with Judah's t-shirt. A little color was sneaking back into his face, but not much. The strength was coming back to his legs, but not nearly enough.

As the Travelers sat on the ground, Matt grabbed the tablets with one arm and Bella with the other arm. He pulled them both close to himself. "We'll be okay," he whispered to her. "I promise."

Judah crawled over to where Jennifer was and tucked her under his arm. Within a couple of moments, everyone was hunched close together, huddling around Sam and the cave. They didn't desire to go back inside; it seemed like more of a grave now than a safe place, with the land rumbling as it was. They still might have to dive back inside, however, if the king suddenly came back around the bend. None of them moved too far away from the opening.

It was not the king who was causing the land to shake; not at all. The king was very busy finding a shelter of his own. Kaija Mae looked to the sky and shrieked. She pointed everyone else to what she saw, and more shrieks exploded from the others' lips.

A large chunk of the sky had torn apart exposing darkness, and a thousand bright Shamar Shailmas were showing through. The Travelers' eyes grew large … their breath failed them.

Simeon, how can we see this? Jennifer begged to know what was going on from her own Shailma, assuming he was still with her.

He was.

Jenny, I will never leave you. Remember that always, no matter what happens. I am with you, he said. *I told you earlier that most of the Shamar Shailmas would have to leave you, however, to go and fight in the War of the Firmament. That is what you see now. They have been secretly gathering all this time. While the Nakah Warriors have been waiting for them, believing they would be drawn to the cross of their outstretched swords, they have instead been gathering above the heavens, waiting.*

The Shamar Shailmas have all been assembled now and have broken through, ready to battle.

The end of Simeon's words could not be heard because a deafening roar was coming from the heavens. Somewhere above them, the Travelers heard what sounded like the blasts of many horns. One came from the east, one came from the west, one came from the south, and one came from the north.

One after another they blasted loud until they were all heard at the same time. The Travelers plugged their ears and watched the skies with great dread and trepidation. The entire air was filled with loud blasts of the horns and in an instant, the skies tore completely apart. The Travelers' eyes refused to believe what they were seeing. Their hearts skipped many beats and they lost their breath … once again … completely.

Thousands and thousands of Nakah Warriors encircled the sky, and each sat on top of enormous dragons. It was the same beings they had seen earlier, the ones Bella and Matt tried to explain to the others. They hadn't understood their explanations very well, but now that the Travelers saw for themselves, there was no doubt this was what they had been explaining.

It was the tails of these dragons that had blinded Bella. The Travelers didn't want to look, but they couldn't force their eyes away. Every Nakah Warrior sat tall upon a hideous dragon. Where a tail should be, each dragon had a dozen dark vipers snapping and slithering and spitting at each other.

The Nakah Warriors ride upon Dergaz Dragons, and they are just as dangerous and just as evil as the Nakahs themselves, Simeon whispered to Jennifer. *Their tails are made of vipers that shoot venom from their fangs. Anything it touches dies.*

All of the Shailmas were whispering peace to the ones they had been assigned to; some offered bits of information and others gave pieces of wisdom. It was only Simeon who gave Jennifer such details, for it would be her who needed to know.

When the blasts from the skies stopped, there was no silence, it was gone. The ground trembled and the trees shook fiercely. The cave that was behind them crumbled into one massive rock pile and the Travelers were thankful they were not inside.

All at once and once for all, everything changed. The sky that had been a brilliant red turned dark, and the lightning that had been locked up behind the skies was released. Those bolts of lightning were hurled to the ground with such force that wherever they landed, chunks of the ground flew up, leaving deep gouges. From those deep gouges in the ground, fires erupted, turning all things around it into burning embers and ash.

"JUDAH," screamed Matt. "Quick, grab that sword and I'll get this one …" He ran toward the enormous sword still strapped to the dead guard's waist and with both hands was able to persuade it to come out. It was heavier than he expected and Matt had to throw his foot back to avoid toppling backward. Judah grabbed the other sword. Both boys ran back to the others—swords in their hands.

"Do you think we'll need those?" Bella asked, horrified.

"I sure hope not," Judah shouted.

"Better to have them and not need them then to need them and not have them," Matt hollered.

The Travelers had nowhere to go … nowhere to run … nowhere to hide. They were stuck out in the openness of this hell that now surrounded them.

With one final blast—which they knew was from King Shrailzhar himself—the War of the Firmament began.

… UNTIL THE NEXT JOURNEY …

The Beyond Solstice Gates Series:

1. Casting Shadows

Where truth exists ... even if no one believes it.

2. The Fowler's Snare

Strength is found when the eye sees what the heart already knows.

3. Perfidy of Labyrinth

Where the only way forward is all the way back.

4. Veiled Sun ✧ Blood Moon

Where the sun gives no light and the moon throws great
drops of blood ... singing of both a great and terrible day.

5. Mist Over Leviathan

Where wickedness of the heart is revealed and thrown into the depths of the sea.

6. War of the Firmament

Where what lies above and what lies beneath,
is nothing compared to what lies within.

7. Chasm of Acheron

Where no eye has seen and no ear has heard all that may be,
when one truly believes.